THREESOME
HIM, HIM AND ME

EDITED BY
MATTHEW BRIGHT

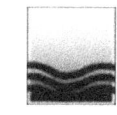

Lethe Press
Maple Shade, New Jersey

Threesome: Him, Him and Me

Copyright © 2016 Matthew Bright. ALL RIGHTS RESERVED. No part of this work may be reproduced or utilized in any form or by any means, electronic or mechanical, including photocopying, microfilm, and recording, or by any information storage and retrieval system, without permission in writing from the publisher.

Published in 2016 by Lethe Press
118 Heritage Ave, Maple Shade, NJ 08052
lethepressbooks.com

ISBN: 9781590212943

The works in this volume are fiction. Names, characters, places, and incidents are products of the authors' imaginations or are used fictitiously.

Individual stories are copyrighted by their authors.

'Strawberries' by Jerry L. Wheeler first appeared in *Strawberries and Other Erotic Fruits* (Lethe Press, 2012). All other stories © 2016 by their respective authors.

Cover Photograph: Daniel Skinner
Cover and Interior Design: Inkspiral Design

TABLE OF CONTENTS

INTRODUCTION | *Matthew Bright*

One

- 5   **CALL FOR SUBMISSION** | *N.S. Beranek*
- 19   **TIME TO DANCE** | *Matthew Bright*
- 43   **SHARE AND SHARE ALIKE** | *Evey Brett*
- 61   **THE BIG MATCH** | *Lawrence Jackson*

Two

- 95   **DR. DAVE** | *Dale Chase*
- 105   **FANCY DRESS** | *Chris Colby*
- 119   **THE GUARDS OF GOVERNOR'S SQUARE** | *Shane Allison*
- 127   **SPRING ON SCRABBLE CREEK** | *Jeff Mann*

Three

- 147   **VANILLA** | *'Nathan Burgoine*
- 161   **INVASION** | *Rob Rosen*
- 171   **SEA GLASS** | *Robert Russin*
- 183   **STRAWBERRIES** | *Jerry L. Wheeler*

AFTERWORD: GREEDY, DEVIANT AND PERVERSE | *Redfern Jon Barrett*

ABOUT THE AUTHORS
ABOUT THE EDITOR

INTRODUCTION
MATTHEW BRIGHT

My publisher asked me to edit this anthology shortly after I told him I'd had so many threesomes I'd just bought a king size bed. (It's not the sex that required the expansion per se, but have you ever tried sleeping three grown men in a double bed? It gets very warm. Of course, if you're reading this anthology, I suppose there's a good chance you already know what I'm talking about. If you don't – take note.)

I'm not quite sure when I became an expert in the field (at least in the eyes of my publisher) but it's a role I'm happy to take on (and one that obviously requires regular research to be up to date on the latest developments). At aged nineteen, I proudly told a childhood friend of mine that I had *almost* had a threesome, having had a drunken encounter with a prowling couple in a seedy gay bar in Birmingham; even the idea of having skirted close to what I considered to be a daringly illicit sexual encounter carried extraordinary potency. The friend shrugged, and said he'd had a few that year already, thus trampling roughshod over the pride I'd felt.

He had form for getting to these things early, having come out as gay aged thirteen, while the rest of us trailed four or five years behind him. True to that record, it was a couple of years before I caught up—which meant there was plenty of ground to gain.

Like when you learn a word and suddenly hear it everywhere, it seemed that every couple I knew seemed to have the occasional "visitor". Most gay men I've talked to had at least one anecdote (though not necessarily a successful one) of an encounter with more than one partner at a time. Turns out a threesome isn't the most daring act of sexual decadence (and it doesn't herald the onset of the apocalypse, as my mother would think if she ever found out.) In fact, it seems to be a pretty common part of the tapestry of queer life. (If you're reading that, sniffing slightly and thinking 'But… but… *I've* never…'—it's not too late! Come and join the party. Photos and phone numbers on a postcard, please.)

Why, though? Simply: threesomes are *hot*. Pornographically hot. There's three of everything in one place, two of everyone else's equipment being waved/inserted/prodded, and a decent chance of being the one in the middle of a good deal of attention. Let's say, conservatively, that gay men are known for enjoying sex: surely its simple maths, then, that the more genitalia in one place, the more exciting? There's more than a handful (steady on) of stories in this collection that are hot and heavy, and all about the thrill of sex, because it would be foolish to suggest that the appeal of a threesome wasn't primarily in the collision of skin-on-skin-on-skin. (I consulted with my publisher about offering tissues as a complementary purchase, but I was vetoed.)

But the thing is, threesomes, like any sex, are never as simple as who-put-what-where. I've had bad threesomes, amazing threesomes, one-night-stand threesomes, threesomes-with-regulars, nervous threesomes, didn't-quite-happen threesomes, threesomes that had disastrous consequences, threesomes that were immediately forgotten, and (thankfully) some very talented partners who knew their way around a good threesome. There's stories like that in here too, in which the bumping of three sets of uglies is part of a story bigger and more complicated, as is undoubtedly true of real life.

And then, at the end, there's some double-cocked aliens, for good measure. What—can't a boy dream?

Matthew Bright
March 2016

CALL FOR SUBMISSION

N.S. BERANEK

ERIC HAD JUST decided not to tell George about the email when the latter looked up from his magazine. "Uh oh," he said. "Are we stuck?"

Nine years older than Eric, he often acted borderline parental toward him.

As was usual for a Saturday morning, they were in the living room. Eric was at his laptop, set up at the roll top desk, and George was stretched out on the wicker chaise.

"I'm not stuck," Eric replied. It was the truth. He hadn't been trying very hard to write, after all; he'd mainly been looking at his email. At one email, in particular.

It's an honor, he thought. *I need to do it.*

George laid the magazine on the side table, carefully, and lowered his feet to the floor. "Let's take a walk," he said. He slapped his palms on his thighs and stood up. "Come on, it's a beautiful morning. Or we can go for a drive. What do you say?"

Driving was an effective way to get the words flowing, but only when Eric went alone. He didn't have the heart to tell George that. "Thanks," he said. "But I'm fine."

"Maybe I can help. What's it about?"

"I'm not stuck," Eric protested. "It's just…"

"What? Tell me."

"Shaw sent a private call." The second the words were out, he winced.

"A private…? That's a big deal, isn't it?"

Eric nodded.

"That would explain why you're so excited."

"Here," Eric said, left-clicking the mouse to open the email's attachment. He angled the laptop so George could see the image that filled the screen: three young men, tangled in bed sheets and each other's limbs. "That's going to be the cover."

It was George's turn to stare dumbly at the screen. After a long pause he said, "Erotica?"

"Yes. Stories involving threesomes."

"I see." George looked at the images for several seconds more. "You're not going to do it, are you?"

"I was invited. Like you said, it's a 'big deal.'"

"You won't send a copy of *that* to your mother, though."

Eric's face felt hot. "No."

"Then why do it?" As if the matter were settled, he turned and headed for the kitchen. "I'm going to have a glass of iced tea. Would you like one?"

"No, thank you." Eric stared at the screen and wondered if he was capable of writing something that would make the cut. *And why shouldn't I be?* he wondered. He was no longer the sheltered young man, newly arrived at college, who'd sat in the student center with a notebook and pen, trying to accurately describe the people around him, only to realize that physical descriptions weren't enough, that he needed to illustrate his characters' inner lives as well. To be able to do that, though, he had first needed to live a little, so he'd set out to get some life experience, to meet interesting people and go places and try things.

It was eight years since he'd graduated from college. Five of them he'd spent with George. Surely, Eric reasoned, all that life experience and a little imagination was enough to inform a story about three guys getting together. But when he closed the email program, all he could do was stare at the blinking cursor on the blank document behind it.

LATER THAT EVENING, George wandered into the kitchen just as Eric was taking the salmon from the oven.

"Behind," he called. It was a nod to the many cooking competition shows they watched. Contestants who'd worked in restaurants always hollered it as they passed through another person's station.

"You're not supposed to say that when you're halfway across the room."

"Oh, I didn't mean it as a warning. It was merely an observation," George said. He raised his eyebrows suggestively, but didn't take the obvious opportunity to close the gap between them.

He was carrying a bottle of their favorite local wine, made from robust Chambourcin grapes, and he moved, instead, to the drawer where they kept their corkscrew. "Dinner smells fantastic," he said. "I'm starving." Eric opened his mouth to correct him, but before he could, George quickly added, "Not starving. Ravenous." They'd recently watched a Louis C.K. standup containing a great bit about hyperbolic teenage girls. It had made them laugh until they cried, but had also struck a little too close to home. "Hey, how's the story coming along?"

It wasn't, but Eric smiled and gave a shrug. "A little rough. You know how it is. Early stages."

George made a sour face. "You don't have to do it, you know. You can say no."

Eric waved an oven mitt dismissively, then dropped it on the granite counter and grabbed the salad bowl and tongs. "Don't be ridiculous," he said, heading for the dining room. "I've got this."

❧

THE NEXT AFTERNOON at Starbuck's, George cut his eyes sideways to indicate something over Eric's left shoulder, before whispering, "Look." When Eric turned, he found a guy who appeared to be in his mid-twenties, doctoring his coffee by the station beside the door. Handsome, clean-cut, and deeply tanned, he appeared to have purchased all of his clothes at Cabela's, while Eric and George looked as if they'd stepped out of the Nordstrom's website.

"He's a weekend warrior if I ever saw one." Eric gave a derisive snort, and then turned his attention back to his pumpkin-spiced Chai, which was still much too hot to drink. "He probably works in a call center. At a workstation, no less, not even a cubicle. He spends his weekends in tree perches and shoots things in order to feel like a man."

"If he had a beard, you'd have an entirely different reaction," George said.

"Would not," Eric replied, but it was true and they both knew it.

"I only pointed him out because he was watching us. At least until I noticed that he was, anyway."

Eric laughed, but quickly turned back around, to check out the stranger again. Partly, he wondered if it might be possible the other man found one or both of them attractive. Deeper down, his gut warned there might be trouble. A man dressed like a hunter probably had a gun; someone compelled to prove his manhood might well be dangerous.

The fellow in question, though, threw his trash in the waste bin and pushed open the door to the street without glancing back. "You imagined it," Eric said, turning back. He breathed a sigh of relief.

"What if he was, though?"

"So you're admitting you made it up. Interesting." Eric lifted his cup and blew on the liquid's surface, but he could feel the heat radiating from it. There was no way he was touching his lips to that.

"Stop for a minute and think," George said. "What if he had come over and started propositioning us? What would you have done?"

"After I picked myself up off the floor, you mean?"

George took a sip of his soy latte without flinching. "Hypothetically."

"Why?"

Another sip, followed by a shrug. Eric recognized the actions as feigned nonchalance. He wondered if George's drink actually was borderline scalding, like his own. "It's just that... Well, he somewhat reminded me of Romero."

Eric fought the urge to roll his eyes. "Larry, you mean?" Larry had been George's soul-crushing first love, a decade ago. They'd met online, in a local discussion forum aimed at fans of vampire movies and books. Eric joined the group several years after them, right before many of the local members, using Meetup, had started holding "face-to-face" events at a local coffeehouse. Everyone went by a screen name in those early days: Larry was Romero; George was GalAdrian; Eric had gone by Thane.

"All I'm saying is that I'm much wilder than you are." It was a reference to the fact that Larry had convinced George they should "do blood" together, which meant cutting themselves open with X-acto blades and licking each other's wounds, while dressed all in black and listening to Bauhaus, in a room filled with candles, as a prelude to sex.

"I know you are," Eric agreed, hoping that by not arguing he might put an end to George's little reminiscence. He picked up his cup, took a tentative sip, and was pleased to find it a drinkable temperature at last.

"It was much closer to the height of the AIDS crisis then," George said. "What we did took balls."

"But you'd both been tested, right? And neither one of you was exactly a player. You weren't out trolling the back rooms of clubs. You weren't sleeping with anyone else. You'd *never* slept with anyone else. He had, but you hadn't." When George blanched, Eric reached across the table and gave his forearm a squeeze. "I'm sorry. I don't mean to dismiss your experience. It's just…I mean, if we're being honest about it, you're more George Gershwin than George Michael."

George tensed, and then pulled his arm from Eric's grasp. "I'm saying I could handle bringing someone else in to spice things up. I've thought about suggesting it, but I knew you'd be mortified." He lifted his cup to his lips but stopped before taking a sip. "All your tough talk about accruing 'life experience' be damned."

※

They were halfway to George's mother Claire's house before Eric once again found the courage to speak. "Have you really contemplated having someone join us?"

"Yes, I really have." George took his eyes off the road long enough to look over at him. "Oh, please. Don't tell me you've never thought about it. You can change the scenery and costumes but it's still always the same two actors, isn't it?" He slowed the car as they approached a stoplight. "And we're visual creatures. With short attention spans."

Eric bristled. He hated generalizations based on gender. "Speak for yourself. I write novels, remember? I have a vivid imagination and I'm very focused."

"Yes, and I'm from the theatre. I can suspend my disbelief, too, believe me." The light turned green. George stepped hard on the gas pedal, causing the car to veritably leap into the intersection.

"You think we've gotten boring."

"Sometimes. Not always. But often, yes."

By the time they reached Claire's street and made a right, Eric was fighting a full-blown panic attack; his heart raced and his palms were sweaty. "You don't really want that, do you? First off, it's dangerous. There's disease. And what if the guy turned out to be an axe murderer?"

"Two against one."

"Or a thief? A diseased, axe-murdering thief."

"It could always be with someone we already know."

"Oh my god no!" Eric felt his cheeks redden with embarrassment. He turned his face to the passenger's window. "I can't believe we're even discussing this."

"You're right," George said, shaking his head. "We don't actually know anyone else I'd want to have sex with."

"It couldn't be a friend of a friend, either. Too embarrassing."

"Well, that's everyone then, isn't it? No strangers, no friends, no acquaintances."

George pulled the car into Claire's driveway. Bright red geraniums filled the white window boxes. Against the backdrop of French Blue siding, they lent the property an air Eric always thought of as Independence Day at the Cape.

Neither one of them made a move to exit the vehicle. "Well, it's p-p-probably just as well," Eric stammered. "What if we found someone and they wanted to keep getting together, and one of us agreed, but the other didn't? There are too many ways it could go wrong. Right?" He saw the sparkle in George's eye dim, and felt a lump settle in his own stomach. "Oh, god. You're really into this."

"Of course not. I'm into you."

He didn't reach over, though, which felt like an indictment. "Just not as much as you used to be."

George extracted his keys from the ignition. "I don't want anyone else," he said. He threw open his door. "I have an idea. How about we forget I ever brought it up?"

⚜

ERIC THOUGHT GEORGE was asleep, because he'd been still for several minutes and his breathing had slowed. He clicked on the program, opened the email and stared at it. He'd read it dozens of times already, and figured he would read it dozens more before, more likely than not, deleting it.

"I was invited to submit a story," he whispered. "It's a big deal."

He realized only then that it was too quiet in the room, that, rather than sleeping, George was holding his breath. "So write a damned story already," George said. "We don't have to tell anyone. I don't believe anyone in your family reads gay erotica. Or anyone in mine, for that matter. They'll never know. And that way you'll be in this publisher's good graces."

"If I write something that actually makes it in."

George exhaled deeply. "False modesty is unbecoming, dear."

"I'm being serious. I feel really out of my depth."

George rolled onto his back, and then shifted onto his right side, so that he was facing Eric. "Why are you so uptight about this? You've had sex before, I know you have. I've been present during much of it." He reached out and playfully tugged at the thin fabric of Eric's pajama bottoms. "Besides, even if you were as pure as the driven snow, why should this be any different than anything else you've written? Do what you always do: Read in the genre until you have a handle on what's acceptable and desirable, and then put some characters on the page and hope they start talking to one another." He smirked. "Or, in this case, other things."

"I guess you're right."

George flattened his hand on Eric's thigh. "You'd do well to muster a little more enthusiasm for this project, mister. You keep saying it: This publisher has asked for your submission, therefore you need to submit to him."

Eric looked down quickly, but found George's expression inscrutable, no way to tell if he'd intended his words to have any secondary meaning. *Note to Self*, he thought. *Never play poker with George.*

"I imagine if you don't submit to him, there will be far-reaching ramifications." In time with the last word, he gave the flesh in his grasp a firm squeeze.

"Oh, good lord. Stop."

A wicked smile spread across George's face. "You're right. I'm sorry," he said, without the slightest hint of contrition in his tone. "It's about a threesome, not BDSM."

"I said stop!" Eric shoved the hand from his thigh. George rolled onto his back and lay there, chuckling to himself.

"You know I'm not going to stop until you agree to write the damned story, don't you?"

"Fine. I'll write it."

"You're not convincing."

"I'll write it, okay? Relax."

"Fine."

"Fine."

Eric closed his laptop and set it on the carpet, propped up against the foot of his nightstand where, hopefully, he wouldn't trip over it in the morning. George rolled back onto his left side and switched off his bedside lamp. They lay in the dark for several minutes.

"George?"

"What?"

"If you still want to try it for real, I think I do, too."

☙

They downloaded but then deleted several apps that seemed to cultivate only a narrow demographic: white, barely post-college age gym rats. At last they found one geared to a broader group of men, and they agreed that whoever it was they finally settled upon, they would meet in a public place. They would go to a motel. They would not bring him home, or go to his home. They would not use their real names. Though they did want someone who liked the same things they did—books, good food, politics, the performing arts—it was only because guys who saw no value in those things were unattractive to them. They agreed they were not looking for anything other than a transient experience.

"How about him?" Eric asked, nodding to indicate the profile that had just popped up on the screen.

"Dale?" George asked. "What is he, a chipmunk? No."

They'd had too much wine. First two bottles of "Cab Sav," as they'd overheard one of a gaggle of younger guys call it during a recent gallery opening, and now a pricey Malbec they'd been saving for company.

"These names aren't real. You know that. We're not using our real names."

"Please. Who would chose 'Dale' for their profile?"

"Lots of people are named Dale. Dale Evans."

"You're not helping."

"Fine," Eric said. He clicked the mouse button. "Okay, how about this one?"

"Jaxson? I'll grant you that isn't real, but it sounds like a porn star. Go on."

Eric sighed loudly. George had found fault with every single profile they'd clicked on. It was almost as if he didn't really want to find someone, after all.

He clicked the mouse again. "What about this guy? Ray. It says he's a country boy."

"You're joking."

"No, why?"

"Ticks."

"Like a twitching eye?"

"No, like insects. I told you about my friend's wife. The one who died right before I met you? They lived half an hour from here, but apparently that's far enough out into the boonies to be bitten by a tick carrying a rare…bug." He paused, and Eric could tell he was fighting the urge to remark on the unintentional pun. "It was awful. She fell into a coma and died three weeks later. She was only twenty-seven!" He straightened up. "No. No one who goes by Ray, or Travis, or Merle. I don't want to end up at a diner drinking coffee with someone who says 'thataway' or 'git 'er done'. I swear to god if that happens, I'll stick a fork in my eye, just to get out of there faster."

"Fine."

"And while we're at it, you can skip right past anyone named Ryan, Michael, or Larry, too, because of my exes."

"Good point. And Claudes or Scotts , because of mine."

"No Steves."

"Why?"

"My brother!"

"Right." Eric clicked the mouse. The guy in the next picture was pleasant looking enough. A brunet, he wore his hair in the still-trendy, center-combed faux-hawk style. His name was listed as Turner.

"Is he a woodsman?" George asked.

"If we're lucky."

Eric was a little offended when George didn't acknowledge his clever remark. Instead, he pressed a finger to the screen, smudging it. "Look! He put down that he lives on Meadowlard Lane!" George reared back and loudly guffawed. "So not a woodsman, after all, but a dairy farmer!" He leaned back over Eric's shoulder. "Pass."

Eric didn't move.

"I said pass! Go on, click it." When Eric still didn't move, George pivoted to face him and placed a hand on one hip. "Don't tell me you're seriously considering *that?*"

"Stop for a minute. What are we doing?"

"Well, apparently you're losing your damned mind."

"I mean, are we really looking or not? Because it feels like we're doing this instead."

George gave an exaggerated sigh, spun on one heel, and dropped into the nearby armchair. "You're no fun."

Neither of them said anything for several minutes, long enough for the laptop's screensaver to kick in and send brightly colored confetti flying around the screen. Eric shook the mouse, and Turner's profile picture re-appeared. "I told you, the names aren't real. Dale? Ray? Turner? Those can't be real. Try to ignore the names." He pulled open the center drawer of the desk and from it extracted a roll of tape and a pair of scissors. Then he retrieved a discarded security envelope from the nearby trash can, and quickly cut a long rectangle from it.

George sat up. "What are you doing?"

"I'm covering up the names," Eric said. He affixed a small piece of tape to each end of the rectangle and placed it over the name field on the monitor.

"Don't do that. You'll gum it up."

"It'll be fine. Trust me."

George came to stand beside Eric. "How's this going to work, exactly? We'll find someone but when we remove the paper his name will blow it."

"We won't remove it, I will," Eric said. "Later, when you aren't here. I'll send him a message and handle all the follow-up."

"And when we meet? What am I supposed to say then? Hey you, come over here and suck my dick?"

A jolt of adrenaline shot through Eric's body. His cock stirred. A glance sideways told him George was having a similar experience.

Eric cleared his throat. "We could agree to call him something innocuous, like Guy."

"How about 'Rosemary's Baby'?" Eric expected him to shoot down the idea and rant until the paper was removed, but George surprised him by saying, "Well, go on. Click it."

The picture that appeared next was of a blond lad with hazel eyes and a polished smile.

"He looks like a 'Bryce', doesn't he?" George said. "Or maybe a 'Cody.'"

"You've totally missed the point."

"No, I haven't. Give me a little credit."

"Fine. Do you like him? Just say yes or no."

"No." Before Eric could click again George added, "I don't want someone who looks like that."

"Why? He's cute."

"So are kittens, but I don't want to have sex with one." That sent another rush of testosterone and adrenaline coursing through Eric's system, but George's next outburst quashed it. "He's awfully 'fresh-faced', isn't he? Practically a child. Assuming he'd have us—which I very much doubt, unless we were paying him—I want to feel good during this experience, not like a troll."

"Hey!" Eric protested. "You're insulting the man I love."

George sighed, then put a hand on his shoulder and gave him a squeeze. "Sometimes, I don't know why you do."

"Look, if he was only interested in guys exactly like him would he have a profile on this site? I don't think so." Eric glanced up and found that his words didn't seem to have had the placating effect he intended. George looked uncharacteristically rattled. "You know what, let's stop. Honestly, I have mixed feelings about this. Partly, I find the idea exciting, but another part of me is terrified." Eric reached for the escape key with his left hand and was startled when George grabbed his wrist.

"No. Let's keep looking."

The next photo was of a man apparently near in age to Eric, slightly younger, perhaps. He had medium brown hair and his green eyes were set off nicely by the burnished copper-colored collared shirt he wore. His smile was just as warm. Eric waited for a caustic comment from George, but none came, which sent a third rush of chemicals washing over him. Finally, he risked a glance over his shoulder. George still had the stricken look from a few moments before, but now it had a somewhat guilty tinge to it. It was the very same expression he got whenever he ate the last serving of something they'd both really liked. It was a look born of selfishness.

"You like him," Eric said.

George nodded. "Do you?"

Eric turned back around and considered the stranger more carefully. "Yes."

"Take the tape off."

"No way! You're looking for an excuse to nix him. Let's just call him 'Guy.'"

"I hate that. I didn't want to say and hurt your feelings. I was hoping you'd drop it."

"Okay then, 'The Guy.'"

"You're 'The Guy.'" George gave him another shoulder squeeze. "Look, I'm still not sure about the whole idea, but take the tape off. I swear I won't let his name be the reason if I decide I can't do this, but I do want to know what it is. I need to know. Not knowing will drive me crazy."

Eric hesitated, and then peeled back the tape. "Ian." He waited, but George said nothing. The clock in the next room chimed the quarter hour. "Well?"

George took a sudden step back. Still looking at the screen, he nodded, slowly at first, then more vigorously. "Okay."

"Okay as in you don't hate his name, or—"

"I'm okay with it if you are. Yes. Okay. Yes." A burst of nervous energy escaped as a laugh. "Let's contact him."

"What? Now? Wait, I thought you still weren't decided on the whole thing?"

"I know, I know. I don't know. I think we should. I mean, we don't even know if he'll be interested in us, do we? But let's see. Let's send him an invitation and see."

"You're serious?"

"Do it."

Eric's stomach was filled with butterflies. Before either of them could get cold feet he grabbed the mouse and clicked the button, sending the stranger the invitation they'd crafted, with a picture snapped during dinner on their fourth anniversary. It was a year out of date but accurate enough, and very flattering to both of them.

Eric reached back and took George's hand. "All right, Ian," he whispered. "Ball's in your court."

⚜

"You're sure you said seven o'clock?" Eric asked, glancing down at his watch. It was seven thirty-two.

"I'm sure." George had been the one at the computer when Ian responded to their invite. He'd been at a barbecue at his in-laws, he said, just about to sit down to eat when the message came through. He was married, but he and his husband had an open relationship, and so, occasionally, he hooked up with other guys for some no-strings-attached fun. Usually just one at a time, but he'd been intrigued by their photo. They'd agreed to meet at a diner equidistant from their houses.

Eric looked out the window again. "I think he changed his mind."

"He said he usually gets off work at five-thirty, once in awhile a little later. He was going to go home and shower first, but seven would be no problem."

The waitress came over and refilled their coffee cups. "Haven't changed your minds about some food, have you?"

"No, we're good," George said. "When we leave, do we—"

"You pay up front," she said, hurrying off to wait on a table full of customers just finishing a big meal.

"I don't really want more coffee," George said. "If I drink this I'll be up all night."

Eric barely heard him. He was listening to his own voice, speaking in his head:

"You're sure you said seven o'clock?" Allen—No, Alex. Or Alec. No, Chris—said, before glancing down at his watch. No, before glancing at his phone. Just then the bells tied to the back of the front door rang out. Jangled. Chris looked up just in time to see someone who could only be Ian—No, Alec. Yeah, Alec. Just in time to see someone who could only be Alec step into the diner.

"Oh my, I know what that look means," George said, pulling him halfway back to the present. "You've got that faraway look in your eye, and you haven't heard anything I've said for the last god-knows-how-many minutes, have you?"

Eric checked his watch again, and found it was a quarter to eight.

"C'mon." George slid out of the booth. "Let's go."

⁂

As he was fastening his seatbelt, Eric cast a look back at the diner. A guy about his own age stood near the cash register, but he didn't have a bill in his hand,

and Eric hadn't seen him in the restaurant while they were waiting. The guy had medium brown hair, and over his long sleeved white tee he wore an ochre-hued jean jacket, probably meant to compliment green eyes.

Eric stole a glance at George, and saw him catch sight of something in the rearview mirror and pause. Then he put the car in gear and they took off.

⚜

Eric was staring at the computer screen when George came up behind him and slipped his arms around him. "Hey, it's really late. How's it going?"

"The first draft is done." Eric leaned back. "I don't know if it's any good, but it's down."

"Good. Come to bed. I'm wide awake from all that coffee, and I'm bored."

Eric let George pull him to his feet. When they kissed, there was a spark there that he hadn't felt in awhile. The uncertainty introduced by the events of the previous few days gave him the sense that George's heart—and his own—still held mysteries. It imbued their relationship with a manageable amount of danger. "That coffee did a number on both of us," he said. "I think we're both going to be up all night." He shifted slightly and brushed against George's hip, so there could be no doubt about his meaning. Then he took his lover by the hand and pulled him down onto the rug, because they'd never done it there.

TIME TO DANCE
MATTHEW BRIGHT

SUMMER TERM: THE PLAN

The three boys surround the table and their arms criss-cross as they pile their plates at their favourite all-you-can-eat Chinese restaurant.

Despite his mouth full, Paul finishes telling his new plan. "Don't worry about the Lesbians. They're in."

"It doesn't solve the *whole* problem," says Huw, "and what happened to yesterday's plan? You were going to start a campaign—said you wanted to bring down the whole school around Mr. Fitzgerald's ears. You were going to be on Buzzfeed."

"I decided I didn't want to go down in flames as a hashtag. The drama queens who caused a big fuss."

"I don't think Elijah's ever been called a drama queen."

Paul plants a sloppy kiss on Elijah's forehead. "Not *our* Elijah."

Elijah wipes away the wet shape of the kiss and buries his chin under the collar of his jacket, chewing on the zipper. " I don't think I'm going to prom anyway."

"Oi—you know the rules," Paul says. "You're doing Shy Boy again. What have we said about Shy Boy?"

Elijah hangs his head—he both loves and hates the nickname. Huw rests his head on Elijah's shoulder.

"Anyway," says Paul, standing up. "It can't just be me and Huw. That wouldn't be right. It's *got* to be all three of us." He reaches into his pocket and then gives them the usual grin. "Who can spot me ten quid?"

Last Winter Term: When They 'Met'
Elijah walked past Rainbow Reads bookshop for six consecutive days before he built up the courage to go in. Crossing the road with hood pulled down and Tom Baker scarf wrapped six times around his neck, he looked up and down the empty street, convinced that at any moment someone from his congregation might jump out and point an accusing finger at him. If they saw him going into the shop, they'd be on the phone in seconds, and he would return home to find his mother waiting at the kitchen table, with pamphlets.

But on the other side of the shop door the blinds were half-closed so no-one inside could be clearly observed, and the calming smell of paper and print was thick in the air. Elijah let out a slow, unsteady breath.

It was an educational first trip to the bookshop, in which Elijah flitted from case to case, taking in the spines and covers with wide-eyed curiosity. They seemed so various and eccentric that he couldn't settle on one title or another without spotting something else to draw his attention. He acquainted himself with diverse subject matters, from lesbian erotica to the history of homosexuality amongst fifteenth century pirates. The only shelf he steered clear of was the narrow bookcase marked 'LGBT + Religion'; he felt as if those particular books might burn his fingers if he picked them up.

Instead, he found himself inspecting a thick paperback called Gay 101. *Flipping through, a small paragraph at the top of a page caught his eye. The chapter addressed various biological theories on homosexuality. The introductory paragraph read, "We all know what we are…"*

Elijah shivered. 'We all know what we are.' The sentence was magnificent, and conspiratorial, and welcoming, and frightening, all at once. He wasn't quite sure if he counted himself amongst the 'we', but he had an inkling that he might.

He crossed to the till, holding the book as if it was a bomb that might go off at any moment. Thumbing through it in the store was one thing, but now he had to imagine taking the book out of the shop, and all the way home. At the counter, the wispy man serving smiled warmly at him. "No charge," he said.

"Excuse me?"

"No charge," repeated the shop assistant. "It's already been paid for. By two young gentlemen. Said they knew you."

"Who? Two?" Shivers travelled down Elijah's spine. *They knew me?*

The shop assistant nodded his head in the direction of LGBT Classics. Elijah saw two boys standing there hiding their faces behind open books. *Spank Me, Daddy*, the taller, thinner of the pair, shook with laughter. Next to him, *Boy Meets Boy*, stockier and nondescript in dress, pressed against him as if to hush his friend. (Friend? thought Elijah. More likely boyfriend.)

"Sorry—" Elijah dropped *Gay 101* on the counter and dashed out of the bookshop so fast that he didn't even pause to pull up his hood, or look for who else might be on the street.

Summer Term: Power Coupling

Ilene holds up the sleeve of some ancient vinyl and blows away the dust. "I'm not wearing a dress," she says, "but other than that, I'm in."

Frankie agrees. "About time we shook this place up," she says, "and screw 'em if they can't take a dick."

Ilene offers Elijah a smile. A friendly smile. "My mum's booked a limo for us, but she doesn't care much where the limo goes. Said me and my 'friend' should go do whatever we wanted. Mind you—she knows exactly how that goes, seeing as I was conceived on prom night."

Huw looked over. "Shouldn't she be all for you behaving and doing what you're supposed to instead, then?" Huw asks questions like this; he wants to figure out how people work, even if they're adults or, worse, parents.

"She doesn't like hypocrisy," says Ilene. "Top three pet hates: hypocrisy, the government, and fish and if you *dare* make a crude lesbian joke, Paul John Woodley, I will break into your house and cut up all your jock-straps."

Paul blows her a kiss. "I'm not a jock-strap kinda guy," he says. "Commando, me. I like to let it all hang free."

Huw winces. "Sorry, ladies. I can confirm."

Frankie sucks hard on her cigarette, until the cherry almost touches her lips, then stubs it out and drops it in the science block gutter. "So—don't get me wrong, I'm all for screwing the heteronormative bias and subverting conventional images of monogamy and relationships, but—"

"Hetero-what?" Paul says.

Ilene shrugs. "She spends a lot of time on tumblr."

"—*but* I just want to get things straight here, if you'll pardon the pun."

"I will *not* pardon the pun," says Paul. "Very heteronormative of you. Probably patriarchal too."

"Shut up," say Huw and Ilene at the same time.

"What I'm asking," says Frankie, "is are you three, y'know, a *three*."

Huw and Paul look at each other, and then at Elijah, who blinks in surprise that he might have to actually say something definitive.

"Yes," says Elijah. This is the first time he has ever voiced being with someone…let alone two someones.

Huw nods, satisfied with the answer.

"Spot on," says Paul.

Frankie breathes out a mouthful of dense smoke. She purses her lips, nods. "Good on you guys."

"Especially you, Elijah," says Ilene.

Paul spins, mock-offended. "Why especially Elijah?"

"Well—we'd called you and Huw for the glitter team years ago," says Ilene, "but Elijah—not a clue. We thought you were just the…" She stops, rethinking her words.

Elijah shrugs into his coat. "It's okay," he says. "You can say it."

Last Winter Term: The Church Kid

The coffee shop didn't have wifi, which meant it didn't have a crowd, especially not guys his age—which in turn meant that Elijah felt safe there. He ordered a Café Americana and took it and his notebook to a table.

"Hope you're not making a bucket list?" said a voice over his shoulder.

"Think we scared Chuch Kid to death?"

Two boy-shapes inserted themselves into his field of vision, and Elijah spilled his drink. The short blonde haired boy cursed and scrambled for paper napkins, while the taller kid sat down unphased. He ignored the mess and put an arm around Elijah.

Elijah knew their faces—schoolmates, but their names escaped him.

"Sorry. This wasn't exactly how we planned." The blonde, setting aside the sodden napkins.

"Planned?" Elijah mumbled.

The pair of them rummaged in their bags, and produced two books that they lifted to their faces—Spank Me, Daddy and Boy Meets Boy.

"Imagine our surprise at seeing Church Kid looking through the stacks of Rainbow Reads."

"Yeah well." Elijah looked from one to the other.

The blonde shook his head. "Sorry, I know that's not actually our name. We do actually know it: you're Elijah."

"I thought you were an Edmund, actually," said the other. "But apparently not."

"I'm Huw," said Boy Meets Boy.

"And I'm Paul," said Spank Me, Daddy.

A waitress arrived with coffee on a tray—a blackforest mocha that she placed in front of Huw and a double espresso to Paul. "And could you bring another of whatever he was having, please?" said Huw. When she'd gone, he slid around the booth so he was halfway between the two of them. "I don't want it to look like we're interviewing you or anything."

Paul grinned. "But we really are. Look, I've got a tick-sheet right here," he said, and then when Huw glared at him, "Sorry, sorry. Joke. Obviously. We filled out the tick-sheet weeks ago."

Paul and Huw both turned their attention to their drinks, and Elijah sat, not quite sure what to say.

"Oh," said Huw, "here." He dug in his bag, and plonked a carrier bag down on the table. When Elijah didn't respond, he pushed it towards it. "It's yours."

Elijah peeked inside, and recognised the pale mauve cover of Gay 101.

"Um… thanks," he said.

"It was a silly idea," said Huw.

"It was a great idea," said Paul.

"It was meant to be like… you know when people see someone they think is attractive, and then they buy them a drink…"

"…well, we weren't in a bar, we were in a bookshop," interrupted Paul. "So we bought you a book instead."

Elijah had just taken a bite of the free mince pie that came with coffee, and he choked, spraying the table with crumbs. It had taken him a few moments to unravel their explanation, but when he had, the word 'attractive' had ricocheted around his head, knocking over everything in its path. He inspected it from either side, poked it, tried it on for size. It felt like a new suit, smart but unfamiliar.

He rather liked the feeling. Which wasn't stopping him choking. Huw clapped him hard on the back. "Are you alright?"

"Yes—sorry—I mean—that's..."

"What?" Paul had an unreadable expression

Once, in the crush to get to class when the bell rings, someone had pinched Elijah's bottom. He had turned, unable to see who had done it. The only possible culprits were a gaggle of those girls—the skinny popular kind who seemed to have figured out how to wield their breasts as weapons far earlier than they had any right to. They were laughing amongst themselves, and distinctly not looking at Elijah. He had felt a cold shame, not because he was embarrassed at the contact, but because what the pinch really meant was that the idea of anyone finding him—the awkward Church Kid with the capital letters, and the bad haircut, and the several extra stones of weight—attractive was ridiculous. So laughable that a pinch on his full buttocks could only be interpreted as a joke.

"It's just—I'm not. Attactive." He almost whispered the last word, like it was a magic spell.

Paul and Huw looked at each other, as if they were sharing a joke—or no, not quite a joke, Elijah realised. They weren't laughing, but they were sharing something he wasn't in on. Paul hook his head. "Sorry, Edmund, but that's not up for debate."

Elijah looked to Huw, who nodded and smiled, which revealed dimples.

"Hold on," said Elijah, "aren't you two... boyfriends?"

Huw sighed. "Kinda. No. Yes. Not really. Let's stick with kinda."

Paul threw back his head and downed his double espresso, slamming the cup back down, making the table shake. "What does us being boyfriends have to do with thinking you're hot? Hmmmm?" His eyebrows shot up and wiggled. He peeled his free mince pie out of its foil holder, and crammed it into his mouth in one go. Crumbs cannoned from between his lips as he chomped. "Don't you think we're attractive?"

Elijah didn't answer the question until much later that afternoon.

Summer Term: The Third Woman

Alice shakes her head. "Why would I *ever* want to do that?" She turns to her painting, set up on the one of the school easels. The room is quiet at this hour—the only people in the art room at this time are those that take the subject as an addition to their other subjects, which is mostly just Alice and the occasional student more interested in a quiet place to spend lunch-times than in art.

"Sounds like a great plan. I'm sure you'll have your triumphant moment—but it's really not my thing."

"Because anyone who doesn't go to prom is destined to be a loser for the rest of their lives… don't you *watch* films?" Paul says.

Alice pokes him in the face with the wet end of her brush. A red streak bisects his cheek; it gives him the air of a wild hunter. "*You* can shut up—I know how you like to talk people into things. I have *zero* desire to go to prom. *Zero* desire to be asked by a boy. *Zero* desire to be asked by a girl. *Zero* desire to hire a limo. *Zero* desire to dance sober to bad music."

"All I'm getting from this," says Paul, "is that you have 'zero desire' full stop."

Alice ignores him, and instead leans around him to look at Elijah. "Sorry, hun. But, well, y'know…"

Elijah shrugs. "It's okay." He isn't annoyed. He's actually relieved.

Huw is flipping through the paintings in her enormous art folder. They are of students recognisable from around the school, though they are never painting looking out of the canvas; they are all turned away, hunched and secretive. "These are really good."

Alice looks over at him, trying to hide her pride.

"You should paint me," Paul says.

Alice prods the red streak with the dry end of her brush. "I already have, darling."

Winter Term: A New Year At Midnight

Elijah was drunk—he felt the sudden loosening of every gesture, as if his limbs were a tick slower than his brain, which was a couple of tocks slower than his heart. He found himself fighting the urge to laugh uproariously. Paul and Huw found the whole spectacle equally funny, though they themselves were only barely tipsy.

The fizzy orange drinks had helped sap away the well of nervousness Elijah had felt upon arriving at Huw's house. His mother had dropped him at the bottom of the drive, and waited for him to wave from the door. He had waited her to drive away before he knocked, and once the headlights had swept over the gravel and away, he reached for the door-knocker.

He knew a little bit about Huw's parents—such as, they identified as pagan, a word which conjured images of black hats and drowning pools in Elijah's head—but was still somehow surprised when they both turned out to be a small, cheerful pair who welcomed him into the house without too much fanfare, and furnished him with drink and cake. "Go through," they said, "the boys are in the living room." And they were, Paul cross-legged in the living room beside Huw. When Elijah entered, the two of them jumped up and ran to hug him.

They weren't the only guests there for New Year: it was quite a gathering. Huw's younger brother and his girlfriend (who spent their time giggling in a corner with each other), Huw's aunt, and a magnificent couple dressed in ornate velvet finery, corsets, top hats and canes, who Huw introduced as his gothparents. (Privately, Elijah thought that they were better-suited to his image of pagan, rather than the jeans-and-jumpers of Huw's actual parents.)

With midnight drawing in, Huw's father knelt to light the fire. He placed a gnarled log in the grate, and struck a match against the firelighter cubes.

Huw leaned in. "That's from last year," he explained in a whisper. His lips tickled Elijah's earlobe. "Cut from the tree on New Year's Eve last year, and kept."

Huw's mother handed out small scraps of paper, and pens. She paused at Elijah. "Would you like to join us, Elijah?" she said. "You don't have to, of course—I know your parents…"

Elijah seemed to have caught some of Paul's boldness, because he found he didn't care too much about 'your parents…' and he took the two slips of paper held out to him. He looked to Huw, but Huw already had his head hunched over, writing.

Paul came to the rescue, nudging him. "You write on one something you were thankful for this year," he said, "and on the other, something you wish for in the coming year."

Elijah chewed his pen for a while, thinking, and then decisively, wrote the same thing on both, and folded them. Then, one by one, they cast their papers into the flames of last year's tree as fireworks exploded outside the window for the chiming of midnight.

Summer Term: History Lessons

Elijah likes being in a car in silence, especially at night; he finds each street light as it passes in rhythm mesmerising, and calming. His mother drives beside him, occasionally grating the gears, and muttering to herself. They are on the way back from the church—her from the Wednesday night prayer meeting, him from painting scenery for the holiday bible club due to begin in a month.

As they pass the docks, he looks over at his mother. "Can I ask a question?"

he says. He rubs his fingertips together, feels the paint flaking off them.

His mother doesn't look away from the road—she's afraid to. Not a natural driver his mother, but she doesn't frown or grumble, so he takes it as a yes.

"How did you and Dad meet?"

She pushes her glasses up her nose, and stares out at the passing of the half-hearted cluster of seafront amusements. "I thought you knew the story: St John's College."

"Tell me again."

"Well…after Bible study—I think it was the Gospel of Matthew, as I remember some argument over using magi versus kings, magi seemed too, oh, supernatural, though these days with everyone adoring J.K. Rowling—"

"Mum!"

"Sorry, dear. Your father asked me on a date. We went to see the castle and then had curry. Doesn't sound very glamorous, but this was Durham in 1973, so a korma was pretty exotic."

Elijah, looks out of the side window. He can just make out the white crests of waves breaking on the beach. A little while later, he says, "How did you know you were in love with him?"

His mother chances a glance at him. "I couldn't stop thinking about him from the day I met him to day I married him."

Elijah nods. "What about *after* you married him?"

"That's a whole different story."

They drive in silence a while longer, until they reach the house and pull into the drive. She grates the gears again, and jerks on the handbrake.

"So—who is it then?" she says.

He says nothing, just fiddles with his seatbelt.

"Is it Alice?" she says. "You've mentioned her a few times. You should bring her over to the house, you know. You know we like to meet your…friends."

He opens the door and climbs out, slamming it behind him and says—not quite sure if she can hear him or not—"It's not Alice."

Winter Term: All The Fireworks

Later, they lay on their backs on the trampoline at the bottom of the garden, feeling the cold damp spread across their backs and legs, and not much caring. Huw lived on the very edge of the town, away from the sea, far enough from streetlights that you could see the stars in the dark sky above. Together, they lay and stared, and at some point Elijah, who was between Huw and Paul, realised he was holding their hands on either side.

There had been a cavalcade of fireworks that lit up the sky in fierce explosions of colour at midnight, setting a string of dogs barking and howling in their back gardens. Then, eventually, it had become still, and they had slipped outside to the dark where there was only only the warm kitchen light stretching gold fingers across them, and the muffled sound of music from inside the house.

Paul was still, and Elijah realised how unusual this was—for him not to be moving in some way, be it fidgeting, leaping, finger-wagging. He twisted his head to look at him, and discovered that Paul was already looking at him, his eyes no more than darker shadow in the gloom.

In his other hand, Huw's finger moved in circles in his palm. Then Paul leaned forward and kissed him lightly on the lips.

It was Elijah's first kiss; his second was to follow shortly after. In giddy disbelief, he turned to Huw, accustomed to looking in his direction for reassurance over Paul's behaviour. Perhaps it had been a mistake, or a joke or…

Then Huw's mouth too was against his, and Elijah no longer worried.

Summer Term: Top and Tail

Huw is making a top hat, which he has told anyone who'll listen is Not Easy. "But I'm pretty certain I'll be the only person with a top hat," he tells Elijah.

They are in the shed at the bottom of Huw's garden (it's a big garden, and there are a lot of strange things to be found at the bottom of it). It is kitted inside as a workshop, where Huw's father makes dresses and tinkers with obscure pieces of clockwork machinery. The small windows are clogged with rain and fog, but Elijah stares out, looking at the trampoline being lashed by the rain. If he squints, he can look further, over the fence at the end, to distant tree-tops— but that story comes later.

Huw is stooped over his work, weaving his needle carefully in and out of the seam between the black felt and the bright purple silk lining. It feels almost strange for it to be just the two of them, like the feeling in a party when everyone peels away until you are left with someone you realise you don't quite know how to talk to. In the many months since the bookshop, it has become custom that it is all three of them—rarely are they ever purely in pairs. They have slotted together into the rhythms of a trio, whether they be talking, mooching round town, or kissing in whatever snatched moments they can go unobserved.

Usually these moments are at Huw's house, because both Elijah and Paul assiduously dodge any suggestion that they should spend collective time at either of their homes. Paul is meant to be here now, but has yet to show.

"You're going to stand out, anyway," says Elijah, crossing to observe Huw's skilled fingers close-up.

"Yes," says Huw. Elijah isn't certain he sounds entirely happy about that.

He lets it lie for a minute, but then it begins to nag at his own worries, and he can't resist. "I mean—why do we *have* to make a show of ourselves?"

Huw smiles. "Because Paul wants to make his big statement, and we love him." He trips over the end of the sentence, but it's too late. Huw keeps his eyes steadfastly on the needle.

"Yes," says Elijah, "we do."

Huw puts down the hat, and turns to Elijah, pulling him by the hips to press against his body. He pulls Elijah by the hips to press against him, and kisses him slowly, opening his lips to let their tongues play against each other. "Thank you," he says, when they stop.

Elijah can feel Huw hardening in his trousers, pressed so tight against him, and begins to respond himself, but there isn't a lock on the shed, and Huw's parents have a habit of popping in without warning. He pushes Huw away gently.

"I'm worried about him, actually," says Huw, leaning his head on Elijah's chest.

"Why?"

"I think he thinks this prom thing is a kind of… last hurrah?"

"That doesn't make any sense—none of us are going anywhere after."

Huw shrugs. "Paul kind of treats everything like a last hurrah."

Elijah feels almost duplicitous talking about Paul when he isn't there to speak for himself—but at the same time, with Huw's fingers burrowing into his jeans pockets, he also feels like he is being pulled closer into the orbit of Huw as a single body, rather than Huw as the quiet moon circling Paul's storm-swept planet.

Huw detaches himself and turns back to the hat. "Plus, and I'd never admit this to Paul, but I'm kinda scared." He darts a sideways glance at Elijah. "Sorry—

it's stupid. I haven't got anything to lose. You're the one who risks being thrown out of his house, or whatever."

Elijah turns a brass monocle between his fingers, like a magician with a coin. "Everyone seems to think my parents are monsters, but they're not. They wouldn't throw me out of the house, or beat me up, or anything. My mum would probably just sit me down with a cup of tea and the Bible, or something."

"Doesn't sound too bad."

"No it doesn't, but..."

"...but there are far more ways than physical for a parent to hurt their child?" Sometimes, Huw sounds decades older than he has any right to. "We know all about it."

He snips a thread, and lifts the hat to his head, strikes a pose, which is when Paul bursts through the door.

Spring Term: Pauls' Parents
"We don't talk about Paul's parents," said Huw, in an aside to Elijah.
And that was that.

Summer Term: One Of Your French Girls
"Watch—count," says Elijah. He and Alice sit beside each other on his bed. The door is closed. "Five, four..."

At one, the door swings open.

"Hi, Mum."

She bustles in with cups of tea on a tray. "You two okay in here? I thought you might like drinks..." The tea is in china teacups, the good set for guests, and there is a biscuit on each saucer.

"Thanks," says Elijah, and Alice echoes him.

"So what are you two up to then?" his mother asks, a little too brightly.

Alice brandishes her pencil and sketchbook. "I'm just drawing Elijah."

His mother blinks like an owl. "Lovely," and then again: "Lovely!" When neither of them say much else, she backs out of the room. "I'll leave you to it, then."

"Told you," says Elijah when she is gone. "Can't have the door closed—we could be up to *anything*."

Alice frowns at her paper, the pencil moving quickly as she sketches him.

"What about when Paul and Huw visit? Does she keep the door open then?"

"They don't visit. It'd be…weird."

She looks up at him, sizing up his shape and angles, then goes back to drawing. "Weird how?"

He struggles to put into word the queasy feeling that thought gives him. "Its like… baked beans in the middle of a chocolate cake. Or a sex scene in the middle of a Disney film. Both things are fine on their own, but really *not* in the same place at the same time."

Besides, he thinks, with my mother, Paul and Huw in the same room, how would I know who to be?

"But you don't mind *me* being here?"

He shakes his head. "Weird, huh?"

Alice shrugs. "Hold still."

"I thought you didn't want to draw us, anyway?" Elijah says. He feels exposed. He shifts.

"Stop that," she says.

"Stop what?"

"Breathing in. It takes me ages to draw. You'll faint."

He lets his stomach sag out, and resigns himself. She can draw him how he really looks. Besides, after Paul and Huw and the night in the woods, he's not sure he minds as much anymore.

The pencil rasps across the paper. "I didn't say I wouldn't draw *you*, I said I wouldn't draw Paul."

Elijah doesn't say anything, but Alice answers as if he asked the question. Over her shoulder, the door begins to slowly close.

"He's loud. I like to draw the quiet people, the ones with secrets."

"Paul has secrets," Elijah says.

"I'm sure he does," Alice says, "but he'd never let me see them. Here you go." She turns the drawing pad to him.

The pencil version of him looks straight out of the page—he alone the only one in all her drawings to do so—and he has to admit, he looks handsome.

"Do you really not want to go to prom?" he asks her.

"Do you really *want* to go to prom?"

Elijah is not sure. When Paul speaks he infect Elijah with enthusiasm for the plan, but then the thought of exposing his life to all those people he's grown up with fills him with dread. And that's before he imagines coming home to find his mother waiting, the terrible news miraculously having reached her somehow.

He stares a while at the picture of himself, and thinks: maybe that's how Paul and Huw see me.

"It'd be a lot nicer if I had someone to go with…"

She sighs. "Yeah, well—I'm not interested any of them. Boys. Girls. Whatever. Seems to me prom is just a complicated excuse to get laid in nice clothes. I don't see the attraction. And there'll be just me in the corner, couldn't care less about any of it all, and they'll all be wondering…"

"It if helps," says Elijah, "I don't think anyone will be looking at you by the end of prom."

She chews her lip. "I'll think about it."

The door clicks shut.

"Five, four, three…" they chant together.

Spring Term: Communion

Elijah had built up a tremendous tolerance for boredom. Two church services every Sunday, one in the morning and one in the afternoon, had taught him every trick for distracting himself. It had become a little easier since his parents begrudgingly moved churches, upgrading the experience from hard pews and white walls to flat-screen TVs with song lyrics over moving videos of sunsets, and to electric guitars and sound systems. But once the third song rolled around, and the sermon began, Elijah knew he is in for thirty minutes of tedium.

As a result, he knew there were one hundred and six rafters in the church, four hundred and ninety-four segments in the faux-stained-glass window, and three thousand and nine bricks on the south wall.

As the final song started—the last two minutes of distraction that Elijah watched slide by in misery—he felt a gentle buzz in his pocket. Trying to be inconspicuous, he snuck a glance at the screen.

'Homosexuality is a sickness and you are gravely ill. Come outside at once. P+H.'

He shoved the phone back into his pocket, heart pounding, stomach suddenly nauseous and in the Enchanted Forest, Snow White is being spanked by Prince Charming because he found baked beans in his chocolate cake.

And then he surprised himself. He nudged his mother, mimed clutching his stomach as if he was sick, and points towards the door. She looked at him in concern, and tried to grab his wrist, but he was already ducking out of the line of chairs and making a dash for the back of the church. Unobserved behind the standing congregation, he slipped out of the front door.

Paul and Huw were waiting for him by the gate, wearing enormous black sunglasses and matching trench coats. When they held out their hands to him and said, "Are you coming?" he looked back once over his shoulder, and nodded. Inside the church, the sound of singing ceased, and there was the chorus scrape of people taking their seats, ready for the sermon. He took their hands. He couldn't have felt more free if they had sprung him from prison.

"I have thirty minutes," he said.

"We know," said Huw, and held up a stopwatch.

"Let's run away," said Paul close to Elijah's ear.

The three of them ran: down the steep hill, through the slush-choked town square, past the quiet shops to the docks that lay quiet beneath silver skies, and on down to the desolate beach laid white with February snow. There, their three sets of tracks wove and curled until they drew together in one place to kiss with three sets of hungry, joyful mouths on the silent shoreline, and on the stopwatch the minutes ticked unnoticed down twenty, fifteen, ten, five, zero, zero, zero.

Summer Term: Let's Go To the Ball

It is only when Alice agrees to the plan that Elijah realises it is all going to happen, and begins to truly panic.

His mother doesn't notice; she seems excited. Proms weren't the 'in thing' when she was a girl, she tells him. It's an American thing, only recently crossed the Atlantic. She blames the television.

The plan begins with three stops: first, Huw's, where Paul already waits with him. (It is never discussed that the car might start at Paul's house.) From there, the car will go the Frankie's house to pick up the Lesbians, and finally to Elijah's house, where he and Alice will be the last to join. Elijah feels a confused mixture of feelings about this: first, a spike of jealousy that Paul and Huw will start their journey together (although his mother has made it clear that she will *not* forsake her tearful farewell to her son and his date on prom night) and a deep eddy of nervousness over the idea of everyone being all in one place, within his parent's earshot.

His mother fusses around Alice, who turns up mid-afternoon in jeans and t-shirt with her dress stuffed in a bag. Alice's mother thinks she's going to the cinema alone, and thankfully Elijah's mother doesn't think to ask too many questions. Instead, she whisks Alice away upstairs to help her with her dress and her makeup, leaving Elijah to pace nervously in front of the living room mirror.

At five to the hour, Alice is led downstairs. Elijah bites down a smile—the dress is pure Alice; it trails behind her down the stairs, diaphanous but not ornate, and whilst it might have once been a single rich blue, Alice has embellished it with almost imperceptible streaks of paint, as if she has plucked the colours of the universe out of the night sky and sewn them into a dress. She looks—

"Don't you *dare* say it," she hisses at him.

He acts coy. "Say what?"

"Don't do the princess thing—'Oh, she looks *so* beautiful' shock-horror."

Elijah grins. "Don't worry. You look awful."

She curtseys. "Thank you, darling."

His mother has the front door open, ready and waiting. "Here they are!" she says. The limo draws up at the bottom of the drive and the rear doors open. Paul and Huw step out, dressed smartly in suits, waistcoats and bow-ties. Huw sports his homemade top hat, and has bequeathed to Paul a silver-topped cane for the occasion.

Elijah holds in a breath. This, perhaps, is what he is meant to feel as the girl ascends the stair in her dress. He catches the boys eyes; they crease conspiratorially as they—true gentlemen—open the rear doors to help out the girls.

Alice's hand jumps to grip Elijah's, grip tight, stifling laughter.

"Oh, my, well—that's… unconventional," say's Elijah's mother.

Ilene and Frankie wear matching tuxes, and Frankie sports a top hat to rival Huw's. She links arms with him and marches boldly up the drive towards the house.

"Well," says Elijah's mother, "you two enjoy yourselves." A phantom *but not too much* hangs in the air unsaid.

Elijah wraps her in a hug, and kisses her on the cheek. "See you later."

"Hold on!" calls his mother. "Let's get a photo of you all."

They gather together, boy-girl-boy-girl-boy-girl, their arms around each other's shoulders. "Smile," his mother calls, and as the camera flashes, Elijah feels someone pinch his bottom. When his mother sets aside the camera and waves them on their way, he looks left and right, trying to figure out who was responsible, but both Paul and Huw avoid his gaze and instead throw open the car door and bundle him inside.

The ride to the school is giddy, full of laughter and music. Paul has a silver flask in his jacket, which he passes between them. The girls pluck off their corsages and hurl them delightedly in a pile between their feet.

"Are we really doing this, then?" says Frankie, and Paul looks from Huw to Elijah and back to her, and nods.

"Yep," he says.

They are amongst the first to arrive, which is also part of the plan. For the most parts the teachers are fairly unconcerned—though Mr. Fitzgerald eyes Paul suspiciously at the entrance as they make their way up the red carpet. Paul lifts up Frankie's hand and kisses it expressively, meeting the headmaster's eyes as they pass.

Huw jostles against Elijah. "Ready?" he asks.

There are banks of pupils lining the red carpet, some disinterested, but most watching as we arrive. Elijah feels eyes on him—eyes he can imagine assessing him, he in his tuxedo and Alice in her beautiful gown, as entirely new people, as if the limo was a chrysalis from which they have emerged. He knows it is happening because he is doing the same to those he catches sight of: over there the three girls who served as library monitors, Chloe, Grace and Skye, who have chosen matching dresses that reveal hitherto unguessed-at cleavage, looking pleased and grown-up; over here, Jostein, the quiet mousy boy that Elijah has shared technology class with for five years without really noticing and who, in purple tie and gold waistcoat, Elijah is surprised to discover he is quite attracted to. He even has to begrudgingly admit that the girls he hates look spectacular in their expensive dresses; it is as if everyone he has known for the last five years has suddenly stepped into entirely different stories.

He lets his fingers trail across Huw's, unseen in the crowd. "Too late now," he says.

In the entrance hall, there is a queue—couples waiting to step in front of the official photographer. On the other side of the wall—hung with blue drapes and streamers—music is playing loudly, and there is the scent of popcorn in the air; it feels almost like a carnival, and the energy is infectious. Paul and Ilene are first in line, nudging and elbowing each other with brother-sister affection that—or so it seems to Elijah—is so blatantly unsexual that surely no-one could believe they were actually a couple. Frankie is pressing her phone into Huw's hand, debating out loud whether posting a picture of herself in makeup constitutes giving in to the patriarchy, and barking at Huw for choosing bad angles.

Alice pulls him aside, and puts her hands on his shoulders. "Elijah—I have something I want to say to you." She swallows hard. "I know I said I didn't care about all this stuff, but… well, I was thinking, after prom tonight… I'd like you…"

"…what?"

She looks him dead in the eyes. "I'd like us to be each other's first."

Ten seconds later she lets him off the hook, walloping him hard on the arm, and bursting into laughter. "My god—your face!"

Elijah finds himself laughing. He shoulder-barges her, bouncing her off the wall, which sets her off laughing even more. "I was going to say… I think you've fundamentally misunderstood some major parts of the plan here…!" The line shuffles forward; Paul and Frankie strike an ungainly pose, her clutching his cane phallic between her legs, him doffing and pouting at the camera, arms spread dramatically. The camera flashes.

"Besides," says Elijah, hiding a smirk, "I could be *your* first, but you couldn't be mine."

Alice hugs his arm. "Well now—aren't *you* a dark horse, darling!"

Spring Term: Lycanthropy

The woods on the edge of town were lovely, dark and deep, and when Elijah said this out loud, Paul spun around and told him he remembered that poem. "And miles to go before I sleep," he stage-whispered, and then began to run backwards through the undergrowth, dodging tree-trunks, repeating it louder and louder into the dark canopy of trees above. "And miles to go before I sleep!"

Then he turned and darted away, Pucklike between the trees, until he vanished away in the gloom. Huw took Elijah's hand and the two followed after him, tracking the sound of his crashing and calling. Huw was flushed red, elated, and vibrant in a way that Elijah rarely saw him. He was normally so calm and studied. "That boy,"

Huw said, shaking his head, though there was no recrimination.

Somewhere up ahead, music began—a high, palm-muted guitar, plucking out a racing rhythm that ebbed and flowed to make way for a woman's voice, cool and enticing. The song was familiar: Time To Dance, Paul's favourite song, one he would often play from his phone when the three of them were alone; he said it was their song. He must be doing the same now, racing ahead of them, the music drawing them onwards like in the fairy stories of the mysterious forces that tempted travellers from the road.

For several verses, the song stayed ahead of them, and then it began to grow near, and soon Huw and Elijah found the phone atop a treestump. It was faint and evanescent, leaking the melody into the trees. Elijah reached to pick up the phone, and turned on its torch function. The bright light picked out a clearing in the woods.

In its centre, Paul stood, his arms spread and his clothes pooled at his feet. Torchlight flashed across him. The half-glimpsed image of white-bathed skin shot through Elijah like static, raising the hair on his arms. The beam tipped away to illuminate a circle of dry bracken.

"Come on then," said Paul's voice in the dark. "We're here—no-one to see us. Just the three of us, at last."

Elijah turned the light back on him. The sight filled him with a sense he could ill define: a feeling that adulthood was waiting on the edge of the trees, and an exhilarating sense of daring that someone could be so freely bare in front of him. It was as if all the rules of what parts of the body should be covered had been broken and discarded with the rest of Paul's clothing.

He sensed Huw's presence behind him, then felt arms rest on the back of his shoulder, and Huw's cheek against the back of his head. Spotlit and under the inspection of both their eyes, Paul grew erect. He spread his hands, letting them watch him. At that moment, Elijah could not imagine a sight more erotic.

Paul walked towards him, his bare feet brushing through the branches and leaves. He reached out and plucked the phone from Elijah's hand. The light spun around the clearing for a second, picking out a series of blurred details, and then it was pointed away from all of them. Eyes unadjusted, completely unable to see him, Elijah felt Paul's naked body press against his front, and Paul's lips touch his. The heat of him, uncontained, was hot like a brazier in the chilly outdoor air.

Elijah stepped away from between them. The clearing in the woods seemed a long way from everything—a long way from the lights of the town, from the windows of his church, or the door of his bedroom, and even further from the eyes of everyone who might watch them; if you'd asked him then and there, he's have said the only people in the world were him, Paul and Huw.

He pulled off his t-shirt and jumper in one clumsy go. Cold air broke across his chest. It was a strange feeling: uncomfortable but liberating at the same time, and he realised that he had never been outside without a shirt on since he was a small child. Paul raised the torch to point at him, but he crossed his arms protectively over his stomach and warded it off. "No," Elijah said, and the light turned away from him.

Unbuttoning his trousers, and pulling them down to this thighs, he remembered the kernel of pride that had burst inside him when Huw and Paul had told him the real reason for buying that book, and he thought about the images of the three of them locked in naked embraces that had haunted his fantasies from that evening forward. He stepped out of his trousers, and socks, and then—with only the faintest breath of fear—hooked his hands in his boxers and pulled them off too.

Unseen, Elijah ran his fingers over the fullness of his body, taking swift catalogue of the bulges and crevices, and relishing the feeling of wind across his naked skin. The song was still playing, the voice singing: *it's time to dance.*

"Go on then," he said. The torch swung towards him, and he could see nothing but the piercing light.

"Wow," said a voice out of the darkness, and then another that said, "You're beautiful."

Summer Term: Time to Dance

Elijah is starting to feel as if the lights are too bright: it might be that the silver flask has done the rounds covertly under the table, or it might the unexpectedly bittersweet feeling of things coming to an end. He isn't the only one, he can tell, not judging by the way everyone clings to each other, and dances so hard.

Alice says to blame Hollywood, and drags him away to the dancefloor to get some air. The boys and the Lesbians pogo away together in their wake as the song changes.

Elijah and Alice hide out in the entrance hall. Everyone else is in the main hall, and the entrance feels curiously empty. Elijah realises that a school without pupils in it feels jarringly alien. He walks the length of the lockers, trailing his fingers from lock to lock.

"Are you okay?" Alice's hair has come loose at some point over the night, and it spills over her shoulders.

Elijah nods without saying anything, and inhales deeply.

"You don't have to go along the with the plan, you know," she says. "I always thought it was kinda stupid anyway."

"It's not stupid, it's—" But what it is, Elijah isn't quite sure. *Brave*, maybe.

"You don't have to make a big show of things," Alice says, standing on one leg and hanging onto his shoulder while she adjusts a heel. "Not if you don't want to. Look at me. Just do what I want, or don't do it. Doesn't really matter. Nobody's business."

She's right, Elijah thinks. But then he also thinks about everyone looking at him, Paul and Huw, and imagines them all thinking: 'They're *his*, and he's *theirs*.' He feels a surge of pride. But the he thinks about they'll say next. 'How did *that* happen? What are *they* doing with *him?*'

He hasn't made his decision until he hears it: the sound of the song from the hall. A racing, muted guitar, and the voice that ebbs and flows.

He kisses Alice on the cheek. "Time to dance!" he says, and runs.

When he walks into the main hall, he can tell the plan is already under way. The crowd has parted in the middle, and when he pushes through he spots Frankie and Ilene in the centre, clasped in each other's embrace, their lips pressed to each other. Somewhere on the outside of the dancefloor, a few of the teachers are trying to push through to break up the banned behaviour; most of the rest are hovering on the edges and smiling privately. Elijah catches sight of Paul on the edge of the inner circle, looking around, and Huw nearby, passing his top hat nervously from hand to hand.

The light spins around Frankie and Ilene, and when they pull apart they beam at each other.

Elijah steps into the circle, and extends both hands out. He thinks he hears an an inhaled breath from the crowd, but maybe it's his imagination. Then hands slip into his and the three of them collide together, three faces meeting in a joyful kiss; inside Elijah's chest, New Year's fireworks explode above an ocean that slides across a silent white beach, and three nude bodies move in concert on a forest floor.

The song builds, and builds, and when Elijah looks around he sees that people are joining them—Jostein from tech class is turning with another boy Elijah doesn't recognise in his arms; Chloe and Grace the library monitors are kissing in full view whilst Skye looks on in bewilderment. Mr. Fitzgerald is doing his best to bear down on them but making no headway in the crush, and all he can do is shout impotently from the sidelines, unheard beneath the music.

Elijah catches sight of Alice by the door, a faint smile on her face. She raises her hand, waves once, and withdraws.

Paul leans in to whisper into Elijah's ear. "We love you."

Elijah catches Huw's eye. "We love you too," he says.

The three of them press together for another kiss. Elijah feels arms holding him tight, though he doesn't know whose is whose, and he still can't tell when, as the kiss breaks and the grin at each other in astonishment that they have pulled off their plan, he feels someone pinch him smartly on the bottom.

Spring Term: Stars

Dark woods but not scary-dark, more soothing-dark, Elijah thought. The three of them lay naked on the ragtag spread of clothes. The night was drying the sweat cold and nipping their skin, leaving behind goosebumps. The phone was off, and with eyes now adjusted to the dim starlight through the gap in the treeline above, Elijah could see all three of their bodies clearly. With the trail of lips and fingers still alive on his skin, he was no longer concerned what parts of his body they could see or not see.

"Can I ask a question?" Elijah spoke so softly the wind almost stole his voice. When neither replied, he thought that perhaps they hadn't heard it, and after a while he asked again. "Why didn't you two just have… y'know… each other? Why me? Why did you add me"

Huw shuffled, his head resting against Elijah's armpit. "It's hard to explain."

"Have you ever been friends with someone and wondered whether you really like them or not?" said Paul. "Or whether it's just that you're in the same place and you don't want to have no friends, so…"

Elijah thought about the other people his age at the church.

"Yes," he said.

"It was kind of like that," said Paul. "We both knew we were gay, but we were the only ones so when we got together it was kinda like…why? Were we just the only ones? Then we saw you in the bookshop."

"Oh," said Elijah. He wasn't sure what to make of that.

"Then we fell in love with you." Huw raised himself on one elbow. "And it's like you brought us into focus."

They lay in silence for a little while, until Paul reached for his phone. The screen lit up, and he swiped his fingers until the music began to play again. Elijah felt Paul's lips kissing against his shoulder, his armpit, onto his chest. Huw's fingers strayed from Elijah's palm across his body, and between his legs. Elijah closed his eyes. He wanted to dance again and wasn't the least bit afraid to ask them.

SHARE AND SHARE ALIKE

EVEY BRETT

I'D COME INSIDE after feeding the horses just in time to hear Jeremy speaking frantically to someone on the phone.

"You're *where?*" He went quiet for a few moments, then, "Yeah, man. Yeah, I know where that's at. Of course I'll come and get you. Just hold tight and I'll be there in—damn. It's going to take a couple hours, okay? I'm out in the boonies here. No, don't you worry about it. It's fine. I'm coming. I'll see you soon."

He hung up, hands shaking, looking troubled. Worried, I sidled up behind him and wrapped my arms around his waist. "Who was that?"

A shudder travelled through his body. "He's okay. Well, not okay, but he's alive. He's in a bad way. Needs a place to stay for a bit."

I went cold. There was only one person I could think of that would provoke such a reaction, and I was afraid to hear his name. "Who?"

He slipped out of my grip and sank onto the kitchen chair. His voice was hoarse. "Joaquin."

"You're joking." But, looking at his hurt, panicked expression, I knew he wasn't.

"Look, I gotta go. He managed to get himself stranded in Douglas. I said I'd pick him up." He groped at the table for the truck keys. I snatched them first, unwilling to let him go so quickly.

"That's—how'd he get there?" Douglas was a city in southeastern Arizona on the Mexican border—not exactly a destination of interest. We were on a ranch in the Santa Rita Mountains south of Tucson; it would take a couple hours to reach him.

"He said he hitchhiked."

"You're sure it's him?"

"Dead sure." Jeremy held out his hand, but I kept the keys dangling out of his reach. "He mentioned things we did at college, conversations no one else overheard."

"That Popeye tattoo on your butt?"

He blushed "That, too."

"Where's he been for five years? Why did he disappear, for that matter?"

Jeremy shook his head. "I don't know. He didn't say. He was upset. Desperate. Please, Avery—give me the damn keys!"

I held them aloft and stepped back. "How did he find us?"

He let out an irritated sigh. "How do you think?"

We sometimes rented out the ranch for weddings and camping expeditions, and we had a website with our contact information. I suspected Jeremy had gone for high visibility in the hopes that Joaquin would find him someday. Now he had, and I wasn't sure I liked that fact.

"Say it's all right. Please. For me. I have to go."

"Jer, I…fine." I let him grab the keys. "Do you want me to ride with you?" Anxious as he was, I was afraid to let him drive.

"Thanks, but I'd better go alone. He sounded spooked." He grabbed his wallet from the counter, stuffed it in his back pocket and left. A moment later, a dust cloud rose as he sped down the dirt road toward the gate.

Torn, I watched him go. It wasn't that I minded guests—I didn't. Unless they were my partner's ex-boyfriend.

※

Leapfrog Ranch was named for the rare Chiricahua leopard frogs which made our pond their home. The ranch still belonged to my parents, but when they decided to retire and travel around in an RV they let me take over and I'd brought Jeremy in the hopes that he'd forget about Joaquin. I enjoyed the space and the freedom of not working in an office and Jeremy liked being so close to nature. We'd collected horses, a few cattle and chickens, and neither of us had wanted to be anywhere else.

Yet even here, surrounded by nature, the mystery of Joaquin's disappearance haunted us both.

I remembered Jeremy's face those last few days of college, stricken when we should have been celebrating our graduation. "He's gone," Jeremy had told me. "Didn't even say goodbye."

I'd held him while he grieved, and while I'd been concerned about Joaquin's abrupt departure, I was also secretly pleased. I mean, if I had to share with anyone, Joaquin was a good guy, but now I didn't have to feel guilty about wanting to spend time alone with Jeremy.

I went right ahead and felt guilty anyway. Jeremy was careful never to make me feel like I was his second choice, but it was an unspoken tension between us. I listened when he wanted to talk about his ex, and supported him when he went so far as to enlist a detective to track down Joaquin. The detective didn't find anything, which only made Jeremy more upset. He stopped talking about Joaquin, but sometimes I'd catch him on the internet, digging. I let him. What we had was fragile, and I knew it.

So when Jeremy got that call, I played the supportive partner while inside I panicked, certain that Jeremy was lying, that he'd run off with Joaquin and I'd never see him again.

The crunch of tires on gravel was a beautiful thing to hear. I went out to meet them, mask of calm in place. Jeremy opened his door and swung down. Then the passenger door opened, and out came a frail-looking man I nearly didn't recognize.

Joaquin was Native American. What tribe I'd never asked, and he'd never said, but his long, black hair, once so thick and shiny I'd longed to run my fingers through it, now lay in a limp, silver-streaked braid on his shoulder. His clothes hung from him with plenty of room to spare and his face stretched tightly against pointy cheekbones. Once, he'd been a beautiful man. Now, he was worn and broken.

I felt like a jerk for assuming the worst. I had no idea what it was or if it would ruin the life Jeremy and I had so carefully built, but something had happened to Joaquin. Something bad. "Joaquin," I said, doing my best to keep my emotion out of my voice.

The smile he gave me was tired but genuine. "Avery. Good to see you again."

"Good to see you too." I held out a hand to shake his. He stared at me for a moment as if not knowing what the gesture was for. Then, hesitantly, he clasped my hand. His grip was firm, but I was careful, oddly afraid that I might break him.

"Come on," Jeremy said. "I'll show you your room."

I grabbed Joaquin's duffel bag from the truck and followed the other two inside. Jeremy gave a brief narrated tour of the house along the way. "Kitchen; help yourself, and if there's anything special you want, let me know and we'll get it. Living room—we have cable—and our room is over there. Here we go. What do you think?"

He took a long, considering look around, then went to the window and peeked through the blinds. "Better than I've had in a long time." He flopped onto the bed, looking utterly drained, and gave Jeremy a pleading look. "Do you mind? It's been a long day, and I haven't slept since…" He stared at the ceiling while he thought. "I don't know. A long time."

"Go right ahead. We'll be around if you need anything." Jeremy's voice was strained, but Joaquin didn't seem to notice. He kicked off his battered sandals then curled up atop the comforter. Jeremy took the crocheted afghan from the foot of the bed and draped it over him. Joaquin didn't move.

In silence, I nudged Jeremy into our own bedroom where Joaquin couldn't hear. "What's wrong with him? Is he sick? Is he on drugs?"

Jeremy shook his head. "He won't say. Just take it easy, all right? I promised we'd give him some space."

We had plenty of that, considering we were on a five hundred acre ranch in southern Arizona that bordered federally-protected land. Fresh air, clean water and canyon views were ours for the taking. "Who hurt him?"

"I don't know. Half the time he'd be slouched in the seat, trying to hide, and the other half he'd have his nose to the window. Every time I asked, he froze."

"He's as skittish as Deuce." Our Mustang gelding had come from an abusive owner and wouldn't willingly come within a few yards of any human, even one armed with carrots and other treats. Jeremy, always the sensitive one, had been working with him, but progress was slow.

"He's got his reasons, I'm sure. He'll tell us when he's ready."

"Yeah." I wasn't so certain. "What if he's crazy? What if we can't help him?"

Jeremy was quiet for a while. I met his gaze, searching his eyes for answers, and hated the pain I saw there. Finally, he said, "Look. I know you don't like him…"

"That isn't true." And it wasn't. I'd never hated Joaquin. I might have been frustrated because he was so often the focus of Jeremy's attentions, but that hadn't stopped me from going to the college café more often than I needed to because Joaquin was a barista. I loved to watch him in his T-shirt and tight jeans, delivering elaborate coffee drinks to patrons. Joaquin was wonderful eye-candy, and it was easy to see why Jeremy loved him. Everybody had. And seeing him so broken and hurt brought a pang of anguish I hadn't expected to feel.

"You always said you were pissed at him."

"Because he ran away and hurt you. I liked him fine when we were in college."

"Did you?" He sounded wistful.

"Yeah." I rubbed his chest, pausing to feel his heartbeat under my palm. "He was the handsomest guy I knew. Except for you, of course."

"Of course." He covered my hand with his, and we stayed like that until it was time to go feed.

⁂

AFTER THE HORSES and cattle got their dinner, we made our own. Jeremy poked his head into the fridge and handed me chicken breasts, butter and carrots. He was the better chef, so I stepped away from the stove and started peeling the carrots. Jeremy cut the chicken into strips and set it in a skillet to cook.

Joaquin wandered in a while later, looking not at all rested. "I know what you're thinking," he said over the sizzling chicken. It was eerie seeing him sit at the table, withdrawn, a shadow of his once lively self. I couldn't help remembering the pleasant smile as he waited on customers nor the quick, muscled efficiency as he cleared tables and carted away the dishes. He was so different now. So broken.

"Oh?" asked Jeremy.

"I'm not crazy."

I felt guilty, wondering if he'd managed to overhear us after all. "We don't think that."

"Not at all," Jeremy added.

Joaquin rubbed his temples. "It's okay if you do. I understand. I'm not who I was."

"We're still your friends. That hasn't changed. So if you ever want to talk…" Jeremy shrugged, leaving the offer dangling.

Joaquin nodded. I opened my mouth to add my own reassurance, but Jeremy's hand on my arm stopped me. I don't think Joaquin would have heard me, anyway. He was staring at the table with a vacant, far-off look.

When we put a plate in front of him, he ate. When we told him to go to bed, he did. Jeremy stayed with him a long time. Jealousy spiked at the thought of my boyfriend in another man's room, but Jeremy returned around midnight, wan and exhausted. "I held him until he went to sleep. That's all."

"I believe you." And despite that little stab of doubt, I did. "Is he okay?"

"He wouldn't say a word. But he's afraid of the dark. I had to leave the light on."

I turned our bed lamp off and spooned behind him. "Jer?"

"Yeah?"

"When we…were you ever thinking about him?"

Silence stretched. I thought he'd either gone to sleep, or was pretending to, when he said, "Sometimes."

I rolled over and didn't touch him for the rest of the night.

⚜

I'D FINISHED MORNING chores and come in to find eggs and potatoes keeping warm on the stove. There was no sign of Jeremy and Joaquin, but a sticky note on the table informed me they'd gone for a walk down near the creek.

I ate and did my best not to mind, and tried not to think about what would happen if their romance rekindled. I'd be the one left out. And how could I ask Jeremy to leave? He loved this ranch as much as I did. But maybe if he had Joaquin, he wouldn't mind so much. I'd mind, though.

Then again, I was probably overthinking things. They had a lot of catching up to do, and maybe if I left them alone Joaquin would talk and I'd be able to wrench answers out of Jeremy later. Maybe then I'd be able to help somehow instead of feeling like a third wheel.

But when it passed noon and there was no sign of them, I went looking. Doves cooed in the trees and hummingbirds zipped by as I wandered down the trail shaded by sycamores. The deeper I hiked into the canyon, the more uneasy I felt, as if I were prying into something I shouldn't. I pressed on, feeling silly at thinking such things. Joaquin had me on edge. That was all.

I should have listened to my instincts and left. Instead, I rounded the bend to find the two of them lying together on a blanket next to the stream. Joaquin looked to be sleeping, his head pillowed on Jeremy's bare chest. The lines of tension had left, but he still looked exhausted.

Jeremy, however, had a satiated expression as he dozed. His fly was open, leaving the remains of his excitement obvious. I froze, dumbfounded and unable to comprehend exactly what I was seeing. Jealousy buzzed through me, vicious as a scorpion's sting.

A moment later came a fleeting, crazy desire to lie down with them, to kiss the man I loved and stroke the one I desired.

Then it was gone and I hated myself for thinking of such ridiculous things. I deliberately cracked a twig. Jeremy flinched but otherwise didn't move anything but his eyes. "Avery."

I stood there, staring at his betrayal, wishing I could think of something, anything to say.

"Avery?" Jeremy said again, almost pleading.

I plucked a leaf from the tree and ground it to a pulp between my fingers. "I got worried so I came to find you. That's all."

Joaquin's eyes flitted open, but I couldn't read his expression. Sadness? Pity? Not that it mattered. I blundered back up the trail, heart pounding. I kept seeing pretty little Joaquin, the way his body curled around Jeremy's, and the way Jeremy had so obviously welcomed his attentions. Angry as I was, I kept imagining what it must have been like, the two of them writhing together on that blanket. My jeans grew tight and uncomfortable as my cock swelled, which made the hike back to level ground more than a little unpleasant.

I took a shower to cool off. They came back to the house soon after, silently agreeing not to mention what had passed. Dinner was quiet. Jeremy cooked steaks over the fire pit and we ate outside, basking in the warmth and listening to crickets and crackling wood. Even Joaquin, who hadn't said a word all afternoon and evening, smiled when he heard the canyon tree frogs bleating like sheep.

When dark had fully fallen, he pled fatigue and went to bed, leaving Jeremy and I alone.

The lack of words went from uncomfortable to intolerable. "You still love him, don't you?" I asked.

Jeremy added another log. The flames flared and sparked. He let the fire settle before asking, "Are you pissed at me?"

"What do you think?" I was angrier at myself for having gone looking for them. It would have been better not to know what they'd done.

"Look. I'm sorry. I shouldn't have done anything with him, but we sat down and he leaned against me, and I…" He shrugged helplessly.

"How do you know he's not sick?"

"He's not. He just got out of the hospital. They tested him for everything."

"And you believe him?"

"Yeah. I believe him."

That was a small relief, at least. "What was he in the hospital for?"

"He won't say. I think he's ashamed to talk about it."

That still worried me. Joaquin was hiding something, but I couldn't tell if it was on purpose or not. If he was on the run, he might just be putting Jeremy and me in danger. "Did he see a psychologist?"

"I don't know, but God I hope so." He sighed. "You have no idea how hard it is for me to see him like this."

No harder than seeing the two of them together—and Jeremy seemed to realise this as soon as he'd said it.

I felt like a jerk. Of course it was hard, and I didn't like seeing Jeremy in pain. Meaning to cheer him up, I said, "I saw the two of you, once."

He raised an eyebrow. "Really?"

"Senior year, in the gym's locker room. It was almost closing time, so no one else was there. Just you two."

"And you watched?" He didn't sound angry so much as surprised. "All of it?"

I nodded. I closed my eyes, thinking of how Jeremy had slammed Joaquin up against the tile wall and ground their cocks together, their bodies slick and wet. Joaquin's hair had been loose and covered his shoulders in a streaming black river. Their mouths had met and they sucked hungrily at each other. Jeremy moved down Joaquin, kissing his neck, licking a trail down his chest and belly until he knelt and took Joaquin's erection into his mouth. I'd been a voyeur, vicariously taking everything in. I knew what it was like to have Jeremy go down on me, and I hadn't had to participate to enjoy myself.

Jeremy put a hand on my crotch and I groaned.

"Must have been a heck of a sight."

"It was." I wanted to tell him how much I'd longed to join them in that shower, to kiss them both and slide my body against theirs. After I'd jerked off in one of the toilet stalls, I'd been ashamed. Joaquin was Jeremy's and always had been. I had no right to intrude.

"I love you, Avery. I always will. It's just…" Jeremy look away from me, into the fire. "I love him too."

My head knew he loved me even if my heart didn't. I stroked his cheek, feeling the light stubble beneath my palm. I leaned in, kissed him, and breathed deeply. He smelled of another man's sweat. He tasted of another man's sex.

And damned if I wasn't turned on by it.

"I always thought it might be fun if…" he began, but he blushed and looked away.

"What?"

But he wouldn't say, no matter how much I prodded.

✥

Jeremy drove the truck to the feed store in the morning, which left me alone with Joaquin. He was asleep anyway, so I took my time doing chores then took one of the wheelbarrows to the shed to fix a broken wheel. I sat on a bale of hay while I fiddled with the thing.

I was so preoccupied that Joaquin startled me when he strode up. "Avery?"

He walked a bit unsteadily, as if his muscles were stiff and sore. "Hey. What's up? Did you find something to eat?"

"Yes, thanks." He eased down onto the bale next to me. "I just wanted to say thank you for letting me stay."

"Well, hell, what should we have done? Let you starve on the street?"

"Maybe." He got that distant, faraway look in his eyes again. "I've done some terrible things."

I wanted to know, yet I didn't. "You're welcome here, okay? No matter what." That last was hard to say. I wondered how long I had before he and Jeremy went off together and left me behind.

"I think I should explain something."

"About you and Jeremy?" My voice came out sharper than I meant, and he flinched.

"I'm sorry we hurt you, but I'm not sorry it happened. I needed that, more than you know."

There was nothing I could say to that, so I stayed silent.

"I didn't disappear on purpose."

"So what was it? Car wreck? Cancer? HIV?" I hoped like hell it wasn't the latter.

"If only." His expression turned bleak. "Look. I know you hate me."

"That isn't true."

"Could have fooled me," he said, but his tone was weary rather than angry. "The last thing I want is to come between you and Jeremy. I just didn't have anywhere else to go." He gestured apologetically, and I saw the underside of his arms. The wrists were chafed and scarred, as if he'd been restrained by a rope that had cut his skin. Jeremy couldn't have missed those marks, unless Joaquin had been more of a distraction than I'd thought.

"So what happened?"

"I was kidnapped."

It seemed strange that a man like Joaquin would be abducted. As far as I knew, he'd never been in a gang or done drugs. He certainly didn't come from a family rich enough to pay a ransom, since he'd made his way through college on scholarships and work study. "By whom?"

"My cousin smuggled drugs over the border. He needed a mule. He figured a college kid wouldn't attract much suspicion. Once he'd decided, I didn't have a choice. They made me swallow packets of coke and shipped me around Central and South America." He briefly met my gaze before finding something on the ground to stare at. "No, I couldn't run. There were guys on both sides. Bad ones. I almost died before the Feds finally broke up the ring. My cousin got arrested. I was lucky they found proof that I was coerced, so I got off after I testified. I was in protective custody until last week."

I vaguely recalled hearing something about a big drug trial going on in Texas. "Damn," I said.

"I don't want pity, okay? I've talked to enough shrinks and doctors. I just want things to go back to…to normal."

Whatever "normal" was. "You tell Jeremy?"

"I can't."

"But…" Anger flared. Why did I have to be the one burdened with this awful story? It would be unbearable being in the same room as both of them, two of us knowing a secret the third didn't.

Then my fury died as I realized why Joaquin couldn't tell. Jeremy was the sensitive one. He'd break down when he heard that story and Joaquin didn't know if he could bear the sight. I didn't know if I could, either. "Okay. I'll take care of it."

Tension leached from his body. "Thank you."

I could tell by his hesitation that there was something wrong, something deeper than just being a mule. They'd hurt him. That flare of anger returned, burning brightly for the bastards who'd ruined him.

"I remember you, you know. Always sitting in the corner of that café on your laptop. The studious one." He smiled slightly. "I saw you watching me. I made sure to walk by your table as often as I could."

So it hadn't been my imagination. He'd been flirting with me after all. Somehow, it made me sad that I'd never flirted back.

"You were always the cold one though, weren't you? Always afraid to get close to anyone, except for Jeremy. I always thought it might be fun if…"

"If what?" I asked. It was the same frustrating phrasing Jeremy had used.

He didn't answer. Instead, he slipped a hand down the inside of my thigh. I froze.

"What are you afraid of? That a crazy man will turn on you?"

"No, I…" My heart raced. This was wrong, in more ways than one. I had no idea what his cousin had done to him, and I didn't want any part in perpetuating it.

"Afraid he'll turn you *on*, perhaps?" He leaned in, and I smelled him, shower-fresh and scented from Jeremy's sea breeze shampoo. All at once I knew why Jeremy hadn't been able to stop himself down there by the creek. It was like I had no control at all, and those urges from college came flooding back. This was Joaquin. The Joaquin. The one who'd been ghosting through my life and was now here in flesh and bone.

The one I'd had a crush on but had never admitted it to anyone, including myself.

I didn't move. I didn't want to, anyway. Especially when he kissed me. His lips were soft and sure. His hand was gentle as he cupped the back of my head, keeping me right where he wanted me.

"Good?" he asked.

I didn't have the breath to answer, so I gave him a slight nod. He smiled, straddled me and slowly pressed me back against another bale. Between kisses, he untucked my shirt from my pants and ran a hand over my stomach. It tickled, but it also lit something deeper inside.

One hand kept drawing circles on my chest while the other expertly unbuttoned my fly. He reached beneath the waistband of my briefs and grasped my cock. An almost electric sensation that rippled through my body, and I shuddered.

I shouldn't have let him trap me. This was probably some sort of leftover reaction to whatever he'd experienced, but his hands felt too good to make him stop. They grasped and stroked and tugged, and all the while he drove his tongue deeper into my mouth.

I tried to reach for him to return the favor but he grasped my wrist and pulled my hand away. "Don't."

Fear tainted his voice. I backed off. He yanked my shirt from my jeans and shoved it up to bare my stomach and chest. He kissed a warm, damp trail down my skin, stopping to tickle my belly button.

"You don't have to—"

But he reached up and covered my lips with two fingers. I gave in.

Hay poked into my neck and back. I didn't care, especially not once his mouth found my cock and he started to lick and suck. His touch lulled me into a trance-like state. At least, that was the only way I could describe the stupor I was in. I couldn't move, couldn't react. He caressed me one last time, and climax hit so intensely that all I could do was lie back and pant while the spasms wracked my body.

When I opened my eyes, Joaquin was pulling on his T-shirt. He looked healthier, and his skin had taken a warmer tone rather than the sickly pallor he'd arrived with.

He saw me watching him and smiled. "That's a thank you gift for letting me stay."

I suddenly felt dirty, as if I was no better than his captors. I in no way wanted to indulge in any sort of trading for favors. "If you think I let you do that just because—"

"I wanted to. Honest."

Our gazes met, and I saw nothing in his face or bearing that said he was lying. "Well. Thanks, then." I had no idea what else to say. Jeremy was going to kill me.

The smile on his face was the first genuine one I'd seen. He gave me a hand up and we went back to the house. Neither of us spoke. The air was too alive, his presence too keen to need words. Once inside, Joaquin retreated to his room. I meant to take a shower, but Jeremy pulled up before I could. I went out to help him unload, and he greeted me with a hug. Then he sniffed and stiffened, and I knew he wasn't smelling horse and hay.

"Enjoy yourself?" he asked, a little hoarsely.

Shame flooded through me. "I didn't mean to. He's your boyfriend. He came over to talk to me and it just…happened."

He chuckled and I relaxed. "Tell me about it," he said. We unloaded grain and groceries, which gave me time to ponder how best to tell him what I'd learned. I waited until he was inside drinking a glass of water before I asked, "Did you see his scars?"

He set the glass down a little too hard. "Yeah. If I ever meet who did that to him…"

Jeremy didn't get angry often, but when it did, it was a fierce, tangible thing. This time, I shared it. "I know who did."

His voice grew sharp. "Tell me, damn it!"

The anger was back, live and writhing like a snake. I knew better than to delay any longer. So I told him.

࿋

THEY SPENT A long time talking. A *long* time. I tried not to feel left out, but this was between the two of them. I'd done my part. It was stupid to feel hurt, but I did.

When Jeremy finally emerged, he looked relieved. "Thank you for telling me. Joaquin says thanks, too."

"You're welcome." I could smell Joaquin on him again, and my heart skipped a beat.

We took turns checking on Joaquin during the night. Every light in the bedroom blazed since he wouldn't let us turn them off. I thought he was asleep, but when I tugged the comforter up over his shoulders he grabbed my hand. "Thank you."

He didn't let go, and it didn't feel right to just yank my hand away.

"I'm sorry. For earlier. I didn't mean to push."

"It's okay. I…" I swallowed, vacillating between truth and a white lie. Truth won. "I had a good time. I don't want you to think you owe us anything, though."

"I did it because I wanted to."

The grip on my hand didn't lessen. I looked at him, shirtless and skinny, and remembered the taste of his lips against mine. It wasn't fair to Jeremy, I knew, but I couldn't help it. I was sorely tempted to lean down and taste him again, to taste all of him, if he'd let me.

I wouldn't, though. Not after everything he'd been through. Safety trumped desire, and I didn't want to risk getting Jeremy upset

He finally relaxed enough for me to get away. "He's asleep," I told Jeremy as I slipped into bed. "He wouldn't let go of my hand."

"Aww. I'm glad you two are getting along." He propped his head up on one hand. With the other, he used a finger to tease my nipple. "I didn't mind, you know. The two of you."

My gut did a somersault. "Well, good, I guess."

"Do you want to know a secret?"

"What?"

He leaned down and whispered, "I like to share."

I stared at him for a moment, too stupefied to speak. "You told him to fuck me?"

"Not in so many words." His hand stilled. "He wanted to. *I* wanted him to. You said you liked him."

I shoved him back and scooted as far away as I could. The thought of either Joaquin or I being used for some twisted fantasy of his sickened me. "How could you?"

He looked genuinely shocked. "I saw the way you looked at us down there by the creek. You were pissed off, sure, but there was something else."

"I was way more than pissed off."

"You were turned on, weren't you?"

"No."

He inched toward me until he was able to rest his hand on my thigh. "Yes. You were."

"Don't, Jer. Just don't. He's been through hell. It's not fair to screw with his head or his body." It wasn't fair to screw around with mine, either. It was a touchy subject, and he knew it.

"I'm not. I swear. He wants to. He says it helps. They left him alone, you know. For days. Locked up in a filthy room. He's desperate for company. He's just afraid of pushing you too far."

"Don't you dare put this on me. Or is it because you think I'm cold too? Did he persuade you to fuck me back in college? Is that the only reason you did?"

"You know it isn't."

"I don't, actually." I swung out of bed, more furious than I could ever recall. I struggled to keep my voice down so as not to wake Joaquin. "I'm sleeping in the guest house tonight."

"Avery. Don't be an idiot. You said yourself that you watched us in the locker room. You enjoyed it."

"That was different." I pulled on a shirt and shoes. "I trusted you."

Outside, the night was cool but not cold enough to wish for a jacket. I stared up at the stars and nearly-full moon, fighting back a scream of rage. Behind me, Joaquin's bedroom blazed with light. An image popped into my head.

The three of us.

Together.

In one bed.

It was what Jeremy wanted. Joaquin evidently didn't have any objection, or Jeremy wouldn't have suggested it. I loved Jeremy. I certainly hadn't objected to Joaquin's attentions, but I didn't want to hurt him. Hell, I didn't want to be hurt, either.

"Avery?"

It was Jeremy. Joaquin was a step behind him, shirtless but clutching a blanket around his shoulders. They made a handsome couple. "Just go, damn it.

I know you don't want me around."

"You're an idiot," Jeremy said.

None of us moved. A slight breeze rattled the trees. Goosebumps pricked my skin. "I'm cold," I said.

Joaquin wrapped his blanket around both of us. He snugged close, ostensibly to share body heat, but his hips locked with mine. "Warmer?"

I was afraid to move. He was too close, and his masculine scent—the one Jeremy had carried too often lately—was making me heady.

"It's all right, Ave, isn't it?" Jeremy asked.

I touched Joaquin's chest, the body which had been used and abused by criminals. There was nothing I wanted more than to hold him and tell him I wanted to make everything better, that no one would ever be cruel to him again. Jeremy wasn't the only one with a protective instinct; he just showed it more often.

I met Jeremy's gaze, surprised by the warmth I saw there. We'd shared some good times, but I hadn't seen him that happy since college. Joaquin had brought that back. So had knowing the two of us had been…shared.

"Why didn't you just ask me?" I didn't address either one specifically.

Jeremy came up behind me. "You would have said no. Much more fun to seduce you."

"Like you did in college?"

Jeremy turned my face toward him. "When are you going to get it through your thick head? I fucked you because I wanted to, not because Joaquin told me to."

"I did though," Joaquin said.

I looked at him, expecting to be angry, and was surprised when I laughed. "Figures. So why didn't you accidentally on purpose spill coffee on me in the café?"

"I thought about it. Would have been fun to pat you dry."

That thought excited me more than it should have. A little of the old sparkle had returned to Joaquin's eyes. Warmth that wasn't entirely sexual flooded through me. "You sure about this?"

"Yeah."

It felt damn good to let go, to finally give in to what I hadn't known I'd wanted. Jeremy behind me, arms around my waist, tugging me against him so I couldn't help but feel how hard his cock was.

I knew better than to reach for Joaquin. I let him come to me, to take his time enjoying what he would, and soon his mouth pressed against mine. He tasted of minty toothpaste, and I sucked at him, hungry to have him at last while his fingers snuck beneath my waistband.

The blanket fell to the ground. So did we, all caught up together in a tangle of limbs. Jeremy tugged off my shirt. Joaquin did the same with my pajama pants. Jeremy pried something out of his pocket. Lube. He didn't give it to me, though. He gave it to Joaquin.

"Trust me," Jeremy said when I looked a bit nervously at our new partner.

He wanted to watch. He wanted to see the men he loved make love. And I wanted to see the men I cared for be happy again. So I let Joaquin adjust my legs until we were both comfortable and take his time lubing me up.

Whatever Joaquin might have lost, it wasn't finesse. He slid inside, hard and swift and sure. I let out a moan. Jeremy cradled my head in one arm and bent to kiss me. His tongue invaded my mouth in much the same way Joaquin thrust inside me—fiercely and deeply.

He'd wrapped a hand around his cock and pumped in time with Joaquin. I tilted my head and he shifted to replace his tongue with his cock. Precum spurted from the tip and I licked it away. Again, he timed his movements with Joaquin, careful not to choke me. I loved the taste of him. Always had. Someday, if I was lucky, I'd get to taste Joaquin, too.

Tension built to an unbearable level. My body hungered for more. Joaquin pushed a little harder, a little deeper,

The two of them leaned over me and kissed, and we were joined, the three of us, and it all seemed so perfectly, unbearably *right*.

Explosions. Stars. All those clichés as orgasm hit in a violent, rolling throb. If my mouth wouldn't have been full, I would have cried out with the aching pleasure of it all, but as it was, I let out a satisfied moan around Jeremy's cock.

Moments later, Joaquin's breath hitched. I felt him jerk, then a rush of liquid heat. Jeremy came last, milking these last delicious moments before pulling out and spurting into the grass. With a groan, he flopped backward, but left my head resting on his thigh, near enough to smell and taste the aftermath.

That was all Joaquin could handle. He crawled up alongside and pillowed his head on my shoulder. Carefully, I curled my arm around him. He didn't flinch or draw away. Progress, then. I was a little stunned at how quickly everything had happened and by how well it seemed to have worked. I felt good. Better than good. And my guys did, too.

Jeremy scooted down and nestled against me. "Thank you," he whispered. He stroked Joaquin's head. Joaquin let out a contented sigh and snuggled closer.

"Any time."

"He can stay, then?"

"As if I'd let him leave." Not now. Not when we needed each other so badly. Besides, Jeremy was right.

It *was* fun to share.

THE BIG MATCH

LAWRENCE JACKSON

Date: *Monday August 24th, 2015*
Time: *09.13 AM GMT*
From: *"Anthony Scott", <ascott1983@mailbox.com>*
To: *"Oliver Grant", <olivermgrant@tmail.com>*
CC: *"Shona Scott", <shosco@tmail.com>*
Subject: MATCH DAAAAAAAY!!

Morning bro,

How was your weekend? Sho and I had an amazing time, and when I say amazing, I mean we spent Sunday with her darling Mum and Dad and 99% of the rest of the time hoovering and/or dusting every surface and otherwise making No. 82 look like a show home in our continuing bid to reassure them we are still happily married, despite the fact we were in Brighton when it happened, and they weren't. Back in the office already and hating the world of Human Resources in a very sweaty way.

But—as my fiendishly obscure email subject header will have already indicated – I am not emailing you about the past. This email is all about the future. Shona (cc'd here, belt and braces) informs me she has **already** coordinated with your better half regarding this coming Sunday and a full itinerary has already been planned, involving not one but TWO John Hughes movies and (I am speculating here) a large bar of Galaxy.

As you will no doubt be aware, a certain piece of silverware hangs tantalisingly within the grasp of Croydon FC for the first time in either of our lifetimes, anybody's lifetimes, probably, even our unborn children, and even if things go completely to shit before half-time, I am willing to get so refreshed in advance that I will remain potentially optimistic up to extra time and beyond.

Are you up for it, and more importantly, what time can you be here with the pizza?

Love to everybody (and Sho),
Ant

Date: *Monday August 24th, 2015*
Time: *09.15 AM GMT*
From: *"Oliver Grant",* *<olivermgrant@tmail.com>*
To: *"Anthony Scott",* *<ascott1983@mailbox.com>*
CC: *"Shona Scott",* *<shosco@tmail.com>*
Subject: RE: MATCH DAAAAAAAY!!

Ant,

You read my mind! Ellie's been telling me I should text you all weekend but then we were out on Saturday night and spent all yesterday watching boxsets and to be honest I slept through most of them anyway. Sounds like we had the better weekend, but on reflection your house sounds a helluva lot of cleaner than our flat. Also pretty sure I'm still hungover – saw my reflection in the staff loos this morning and nearly jumped out my skin. Look like a killer lumberjack.

Anyway, yes I will be there and yes, I shall bringeth the pizza henceforth. Kick-off's at three, so what say I get there at two? Shona, how does that square with you?

As for the City of Croydon's chances, never say never. Aitchison's the best thing they ever did, and he's just getting better and better. Whatever Martins says. Martins says a whole lot of stuff about Croydon and he never saw them getting in an inch of where they are next week.

Super excited about next Monday. Roll on next weekend!

OMG

Date: *Monday August 24th, 2015*
Time: *09.34 AM GMT*
From: *"Anthony Scott", <ascott1983@mailbox.com>*
To: *"Oliver Grant", <olivermgrant@tmail.com>*
CC: *"Shona Scott", <shosco@tmail.com>*
Subject: RE: MATCH DAAAAAAAY!!

Alright! It's on! And I don't care who knows it!

Two o'clock sounds good to me, don't be late (again) or I will devise a penalty.

Martins always talks shit, but I believe every word he writes all the same. Maybe I'm a glutton for punishment, maybe I'm a realist.

Countdown to match day starts now. I'll have to get Sho to wash my lucky y-fronts. Unless she's already burned them, as has been promised many times but never successfully executed.

Big love to all, especially the beautiful Ellie,
Ant

Date: *Monday August 24th, 2015*
Time: *13.45 PM GMT*
From: *"Shona Scott", <shosco@tmail.com>*
To: *"Anthony Scott", <ascott1983@mailbox.com>, "Oliver Grant", <olivermgrant@tmail.com>*
Subject: RE: MATCH DAAAAAAAY!!

Hello you two funny boys, glad to see you're both working hard.

Ant, remember Brighton was your bright idea, so technically it's your fault plus karma you had to clean the bathroom this weekend.

>> so what say I get there at two? Shona, how does that square with you?

Two o'clock sounds great to me. Ellie and I have lots to talk about before Lauren rocks up, but don't tell Lauren that, as plenty of it will revolve around her.

I actually think the pair of you are looking forward to watching your team lose more than me and the girls are to enjoying some excellent movie entertainment and intelligent conversation (makes a change) for which we will actually require no alcoholic enhancement at all. We just do it to be social.

What's the likelihood of the pair of you drowning your sorrows for nine hours after the whistle blows, and should I make arrangements to stay over at yours to avoid A Bit of a Scene, Ollie?

Sho
x

Date: *Monday August 24th, 2015*
Time: *15.05 PM GMT*
From: *"Oliver Grant", <olivermgrant@tmail.com>*
To: *"Anthony Scott", <ascott1983@mailbox.com>, "Shona Scott", <shosco@tmail.com>*

Subject: RE: MATCH DAAAAAAAY!!

Much as I resent the idea that Ant and myself can't handle our refreshment intake, and on the Lord's day as well, I've just had a text from Ellie who says it's a great idea and why didn't she think of it, and is it possible you could just move in permanently? Haha!

Ant, that means I'm bringing my toothbrush. It also means you're cooking me breakfast the morning after.

Dem's the rules.

OMG

Date: *Monday August 24th, 2015*
Time: *15.06 PM GMT*
From: *"Anthony Scott", <ascott1983@mailbox.com>*
To: *"Oliver Grant", <olivermgrant@tmail.com>*
Subject: RE: MATCH DAAAAAAAY!!

>> *also means you're cooking me breakfast the morning after.*

Ha!

Only if I get a full repeat of last time...

Ant

Date: *Monday August 24th, 2015*
Time: *15.08 PM GMT*
From: *"Oliver Grant", <olivermgrant@tmail.com>*
To: *"Anthony Scott", <ascott1983@mailbox.com>,*
Subject: RE: MATCH DAAAAAAAY!!

>>>> *also means you're cooking me breakfast the morning after.*

>>*Only if I get a full repeat of last time...*

It's all I've been thinking about since this morning.

O

Date: *Monday August 24th, 2015*
Time: *15.09 PM GMT*
From: *"Anthony Scott", <ascott1983@mailbox.com>*
To: *"Oliver Grant", <olivermgrant@tmail.com>*
Subject: RE: MATCH DAAAAAAAY!!

\>>>>>> *also means you're cooking me breakfast the morning after.*

\>>>>Only if I get a full repeat of last time...

\>>It's all I've been thinking about since this morning.

Yeah, bro, but now you're staying over. Which means we get to do it twice. Can you take the pace?

A

Date: *Monday August 25th, 2015*
Time: *15.09 PM GMT*
From: *"Oliver Grant", <olivermgrant@tmail.com>*
To: *"Anthony Scott", <ascott1983@mailbox.com>,*
Subject: RE: MATCH DAAAAAAAY!!

>>>>>>>> *also means you're cooking me breakfast the morning after.*

>>>>>>*Only if I get a full repeat of last time...*

>>>>*It's all I've been thinking about since this morning.*

>>*Yeah, bro, but now you're staying over. Which means we get to do it*
>>*twice. Can you take the pace?*

Only twice? Jesus, you underestimate how much I've been thinking about you since February, man. Trust me, it's been hard. Really fucking hard.

Date: *Monday August 25th, 2015*
Time: *15.10 PM GMT*
From: *"Anthony Scott", <ascott1983@mailbox.com>*
To: *"Oliver Grant", <olivermgrant@tmail.com>*
Subject: RE: MATCH DAAAAAAAY!!

LOL, was that intentional?

Date: *Monday August 25th, 2015*
Time: *15.12 PM GMT*
From: *"Oliver Grant", <olivermgrant@tmail.com>*
To: *"Anthony Scott", <ascott1983@mailbox.com>,*
Subject: RE: MATCH DAAAAAAAY!!

Totally fucking intentional. This is what you've driven me to, mate, bad puns. I only do bad puns when I really, really need to get fucked. Tell the truth, it's a good thing I'm not gay because I would have blunted my sense of humour pretty fatally by now.

I mean, fucking hell I didn't even have a proper picture of you. Well, except the ones on Facebook from some fucking awful looking festival from three years ago, the ones where you've got your shirt off and not much on, and you've got mud spattered all up your belly and chest. Mmm.

And your beard was rubbish three years ago.

Date: *Monday August 25th, 2015*
Time: *15.15 PM GMT*
From: *"Anthony Scott", <ascott1983@mailbox.com>*
To: *"Oliver Grant", <olivermgrant@tmail.com>*
Subject: RE: MATCH DAAAAAAAY!!

Just spat tea over my keyboard.

I'm laughing, mate, but I also really badly need Sunday to come right now.

I need to see you on your knees, looking up at me the way you do, with perspiration in your hair, and goose-pimples on your chest.

I really need to feel your skin on my skin, and to hear those noises you made, and you know the noises I mean. I really want to hear it coming from the back of your throat, I want to hear you losing it.

Date: *Monday August 25th, 2015*
Time: *15.18 PM GMT*
From: *"Shona Scott", <shosco@tmail.com>*
To: *"Anthony Scott", <ascott1983@mailbox.com>, "Oliver Grant", <olivermgrant@tmail.com>*
CC: *"Niall Corgan", <ncorgan1993@xymail.com>*
Subject: RE: MATCH DAAAAAAAY!!

>>*Ant, that means I'm bringing my toothbrush. It also means you're cooking*
>>*me breakfast the morning after.*

If you know what's good for you, Ollie, I wouldn't trust Ant with the preparation of anything meant to be eaten by humans. Trust me. I have been down that path, LOL. Let's just say you'll need that toothbrush.

Meanwhile, Ellie's having me and Lauren to stay now and we're visiting the Tate on Monday so all looking like good fun.

I'm just copying in a pal from work who I mentioned your Sunday hi-jinks to and sounded interested. Niall said he was expecting to watch the match on his own and quite frankly I think it'd be good for you to have some supervision, especially given how recently I hoovered that rug in the living room, not to mention had that double glazing fitted LOL. He's hilarious and you'll love him.

Don't thank me;
Sho
x

Date: *Monday August 25th, 2015*
Time: *15.18 PM GMT*
From: *"Anthony Scott", <ascott1983@mailbox.com>,*
To: *"Oliver Grant", <olivermgrant@tmail.com>*
CC: *"Niall Corgan", <ncorgan1993@xymail.com>*
Subject: RE: MATCH DAAAAAAAY!!

Oh, FFS.

Jesus, mate, I really needed to get my tongue around your hard dick this weekend.

Date: *Monday August 25th, 2015*
Time: *15.18 PM GMT*
From: *"Anthony Scott", <ascott1983@mailbox.com>,*
To: *"Oliver Grant", <olivermgrant@tmail.com>*
CC: *"Niall Corgan", <ncorgan1993@xymail.com>*
Subject: RE: MATCH DAAAAAAAY!!

Shit! Sorry, Niall, that message was supposed to be for Olly only. Private joke.

Looking forward to meeting you, mate.

Date: *Monday August 25th, 2015*
Time: *16.25 PM GMT*
From: *"Niall Corgan", <ncorgan1993@xymail.com>*
To: *"Anthony Scott", <ascott1983@mailbox.com>, "Oliver Grant", <olivermgrant@tmail.com>*
Subject: RE: MATCH DAAAAAAAY!!

Hey, no worries, Ant, gave me a good laugh after I got over the initial state of shock.

Look, I don't want to interrupt the pair of you having a catch-up, and you don't know me from Adam. Just cos me and Sho get on really well in the office, it doesn't mean I can invite myself over. Let's all of us just go for a drink some other time.

Besides, from what Sho's read out of your email convo, we're rooting for different teams. Awkward! Although I will concede that Aitchison has been dynamite this season.

A
x

Date: *Monday August 25th, 2015*
Time: *16.33 PM GMT*
From: *"Anthony Scott", <ascott1983@mailbox.com>,*
To: *"Oliver Grant", <olivermgrant@tmail.com>*
Subject: RE: MATCH DAAAAAAAY!!

Did I actually get away with that? He really thought it was just a joke?

Jesus, I've been sweating like a you-know-what for the past hour. My shirt's sticking to me.

From: *"Oliver Grant", <olivermgrant@tmail.com>*
To: *"Anthony Scott", <ascott1983@mailbox.com>,*
Date: *Monday August 25th, 2015*
Time: *16.33 PM GMT*
To: Subject: RE: MATCH DAAAAAAAAY!!

Yeah, somehow I think you got away with it, by the grace of God. Also, I think he's just a really nice bloke who let you off the hook.

Having said that, I think we're gonna have to just invite him over.

Also, I like the thought of you sweaty. Wanna get stuck into that.

From: *"Anthony Scott", <ascott1983@mailbox.com>,*
To: *"Oliver Grant", <olivermgrant@tmail.com>*
Date: *Monday August 25th, 2015*
Time: *16.48 PM GMT*
Subject: RE: MATCH DAAAAAAAY!!

I want that too, mate. But it's not gonna happen if we have him around. You just know it's not.

Plus, we'll have to talk about sodding football all afternoon. We'll actually have to watch the fucking game. I'll need three beers just to get through that.

He's talked his way out of it for us. And I can't stand not to feel you, taste you, especially not if you're just gonna be there, sat next me on the settee for fuck knows how long a football match lasts. I'll have to sit with a cushion in my lap all afternoon. I could do with one now.

I'll email him tomorrow.

Date: *Tuesday August 26th, 2015*
Time: *09.10 PM GMT*
From: *"Anthony Scott", <ascott1983@mailbox.com>,*
To: *"Oliver Grant", <olivermgrant@tmail.com>*
Subject: Sunday Meeting

Okay, forget about that. I tried to tell Sho about my decision last night while I was making dinner, and she got on my case like Sherlock fucking Holmes.

She says Niall just broke up with someone at the weekend, so he 'really needs this' and we can give him something she can't. Which I suppose is kind of true from her perspective. You can't exactly mend a bloke's broken heart by taking him round your girlfriend's and making him watch *Pretty in Pink*.

So, I'm afraid that's it settled. Short of an act of God destroying the pitch on Saturday night, we're watching the game and eating pizza and that's it.

Date: *Tuesday August 26th, 2015*
Time: *09.30 PM GMT*
From: *"Oliver Grant", <olivermgrant@tmail.com>*
To: *"Anthony Scott", <ascott1983@mailbox.com>,*
Subject: Sunday Meeting

Relax, I'm still staying over, right?

Let's get through the afternoon with Niall, let him catch his bus, and we'll take it from there.

Or rather, I can take you. Or something. Fuck knows how blokes talk about this sort of thing when they do it on a regular basis.

OMG

Date: *Tuesday August 26th, 2015*
Time: *09.10 PM GMT*
From: *"Anthony Scott", <ascott1983@mailbox.com>,*
To: *"Niall Corgan", <ncorgan1993@xymail.com>*, *"Oliver Grant", <olivermgrant@tmail.com>*
Subject: RE: MATCH DAAAAAAAAY!!

>>Look, I don't want to interrupt the pair of you having a catch-up,

No way, mate! Sho's said too many good things about you for me to pass up this chance of meeting you.

What time can you get here? Olly's coming at two and we'll be steaming by half three so you pay's your money and takes your choice!

Bless you for saying that about Aitchison. You can be justifiably proud of Reeves. Never had a bad game. He's on better form than ever as he gets older, I could watch him for hours.

Hope you like pizza,
Ant

D ate: *Tuesday August 26th, 2015*
Time: *10.30 PM GMT*
From: *"Niall Corgan", <ncorgan1993@xymail.com>,*
To: *"Anthony Scott", <ascott1983@mailbox.com>, "Oliver Grant", <olivermgrant@tmail.com>*
Subject: RE: MATCH DAAAAAAAY!!

Oh, that's wicked. I was looking forward to a Sunday of picking the petals off flowers, so this is a total asskicking reprieve. Plus, Shona really doesn't have a bad word to say about either of you. She says she's sure I'll fit in, so fingers crossed I don't mess things up!

I guess she mentioned about me and Ally, to you at least, Ant. I'm still feeling pretty bad about that and will be glad to watch the game. If you want to go off upstairs and take care of Ollie's dick, Ant, I'm happy to leave you both to it for an hour. Don't make too much noise, though, okay?

>>*Bless you for saying that about Aitchison. I think you can be justifiably*
>>*proud of Reeve after all this time. Never had a bad game. Worth every*
>>*penny.*

You know more about my team than I do. Better get online and do some research. Always been a fan of Reeves, though.

See you Sunday,
N

Date: *Tuesday August 26th, 2015*
Time: *11.00 PM GMT*
From: *"Oliver Grant", <olivermgrant@tmail.com>*
To: *"Anthony Scott", <ascott1983@mailbox.com>, "Niall Corgan", <ncorgan1993@xymail.com>,*
Subject: RE: MATCH DAAAAAAAAY!!

Hey Niall,

Good to 'meet' you! Thought I should properly introduce myself since we managed to get so personal so fast.

Also, just wanted to make it clear about the dick joke, which really was a joke. I know you were probably joking again on top of everything else, but it's really hard to tell on email sometimes, so I thought I'd check!

Also just wanted to check you haven't shared that stupid joke about dick with Shona yet, as she'll probably tell my wife (Ellie, mentioned above) and then neither of us will hear the end of it when it wasn't even Comedy Store material in the first place!

Trust me, it's not like she doesn't have form in this area. Last summer, the four of us went to Brighton for the day, and I don't know if you're aware but there's a nudist beach down by the Marina. Of course, being lads and having sunk a couple of pints earlier in the day, also you remember how scorching it was last July – not the whole of July, but there was this weekend when it was just unbelievable – Ant and I dared one another to go the full Monty. It was the best fun, truly hilarious. Anyway, we were sunbathing while the girls went off for a walk, because we were 'being gay' apparently!

Well, Ellie never stops going on about how the pair of us looked so guilty when they came back, as if something had happened, which obviously nothing had or ever would have done. They insisted they could tell that I still had a hard-on, when in fact I'm just very well-endowed, as any of them will otherwise testify!

In fact, come to think of it, that's probably where our private joke came from!

Sorry to hear about your gf moving on. We'll sort that with some beers, pizza, and a sound thrashing on Sunday afternoon.

All the best,
Ollie

Date: *Tuesday August 26th, 2015*
Time: *11.15 PM GMT*
From: *"Niall Corgan", <ncorgan1993@xymail.com>,*
To: *"Anthony Scott", <ascott1983@mailbox.com>, "Oliver Grant", <olivermgrant@tmail.com>*
Subject: RE: MATCH DAAAAAAAY!!

Hi Ollie,

Nice to meet you too. Really looking forward to Sunday now.

That's a great story. Yes, I've been to that beach once or twice myself. It's really good when you feel you can let go and be yourself, especially with friends.

Sorry, should have been clear about Ally, not that it makes any difference, but he's a bf, not a gf. Actually, come to think of it he's neither of them anymore. Certainly not mine. I'm free and single once more.

Don't worry, I didn't say anything to Shona about dick. I didn't want her to think that was why I wanted to come over. Not that you're not both pretty hot, but I don't want to get anyone in trouble. Happy just to kick back and unwind for the afternoon.

Just for reference, I've attached a couple of photos of myself.

See you Sunday,
N

Date: *Wednesday August 27th, 2015*
Time: *09.09 PM GMT*
From: *"Anthony Scott", <ascott1983@mailbox.com>,*
To: *"Niall Corgan", <ncorgan1993@xymail.com>*, *"Oliver Grant", <olivermgrant@tmail.com>*
Subject: RE: MATCH DAAAAAAAY!!

Hi Niall,

Just checking – did you mean to send those particular photos?

Yours,
A

Date: *Wednesday August 27th, 2015*
Time: *09.09 PM GMT*
From: *"Niall Corgan", <ncorgan1993@xymail.com>,*
To: *"Anthony Scott", <ascott1983@mailbox.com>, "Oliver Grant", <olivermgrant@tmail.com>*
Subject: RE: MATCH DAAAAAAAY!!

Morning Ant,

Yeah, pretty much. What do you think?

N

Date: *Wednesday August 27th, 2015*
Time: *10.09 PM GMT*
From: *"Anthony Scott", <ascott1983@mailbox.com>,*
To: *"Niall Corgan", <ncorgan1993@xymail.com>*, *"Oliver Grant", <olivermgrant@tmail.com>*
Subject: A Request

Do you fancy staying over?

A

Date: *Friday August 28th, 2015*
Time: *09.10 PM GMT*
From: *"Shona Scott", <shosco@tmail.com>*
To: *"Ellie Grant", <e.n.grant@ tmail.com>*
Subject: RE: Girl's Night In

Hi love,

Young Niall's been smiling at me all morning and I'm fairly sure I know why. Took a fair bit of planning, and some pressure applied on Monday night, but I think it was worth it.

Couldn't afford for this Sunday to get cancelled. Fuck, but it's been ages since I got my hands on you. I'm more than ready for this, believe me. Like I said, I'm good at planning.

I just wish there was more football on the telly, to be honest.

Sho
x

TWO

DR. DAVE

DALE CHASE

W E'RE HAVING BREAKFAST on our little patio and the idea of three way sex with Rudy's dentist arrives like an intruder which makes no sense as I've always agreed that Dr. Dave, as we call him, is a hunk. On my checkups he pops in for a quick exam and I start getting hard which he never notices because he's inside my mouth. Well, his fingers are and his little tools poking around. He should be a model, or no, a porn star. Dark-haired, tanned, and put together perfectly. It makes me almost hate having good teeth. Rudy's are a mess, thus his extended visits which have lasted nearly a year. Every tooth in his head will be crowned. The last one is due to be finished in a couple days.

"You're shitting me," I say. Rudy has a habit for hyperbole that I both adore and gnash teeth over (no pun intended).

"Nope," says Rudy.

"Dave Malone? Your dentist?"

Rudy laughs. "*Our* dentist. You see him too."

"No, I see his hygienist twice a year. You've got a mouthful of crowns. You're…well, I guess I can say *intimate*—now—with the guy."

"Well, I won't be seeing so much of him after Tuesday."

"Whose idea is it?"

"His."

I stuff a chunk of cinnamon raisin bagel into my mouth to avoid further comment because this is happening a bit too fast. And yet, I find I'm not opposed to the possibility. When I glance at Rudy he's beaming because he knows me well. Twelve years in an ideal relationship, open with agreed-upon limits. We each have a boyfriend and the agreement is to see them on the same nights so nobody sits home alone. He has Skip who runs a card shop in the Castro; I have Tom, a house painter who owns his own business. We've never brought anyone into our bed, though we do talk about our boyfriends which makes our sex all the hotter. Tom allows things Rudy doesn't and I get turned on at the idea of Skip's cock getting in where I do. It's a fine arrangement and we always talk about it with enthusiasm. We have at times played around with the idea of a third party in bed with us, but it's always been while watching some movie. Pull the actor off the screen and under the covers. Pure fantasy.

"And you're for it?"

Rudy shrugs and giggles. He's so cute, my little hairdresser, and I get how Dr. Dave would want to do him. I'll admit I wouldn't mind fucking Dr. Dave, but with Rudy there too? It sounds like one of those things that can be either fabulous or complete disaster. "That's a yes, I take it?"

"I think so, Rudy says. "How about you?"

I blow out a sigh. "Well, he is a hunk, but there's orchestration with such a thing."

"No," says Rudy, "not at all. We just get naked and go for it. Totally free. Devour each other, fucking, sucking, probing, prodding, all at once. I see us in a pile, bodies writhing!"

"That does sound good. Okay, set it up when you see him Tuesday. Make it for Saturday."

Friday nights are date nights, Rudy seeing Skip, me with Tom. This Friday I'm voracious and it doesn't go unnoticed. After a couple hours Tom remarks on it. We lie splayed and sweaty, me on my back, him on his side, fingering my tit. "Whatever's gotten into you, I'm for it," he says.

"Thoughts of you," I lie and he beams. It's so easy to keep him happy. In reality I'm thinking ahead to the threesome. It's Dr. Dave who's gotten into me because I find myself wanting it now, him fucking me while I fuck Rudy. I start to picture a fuck train and roll Tom over and eat his ass out. His words slip past me as I feed. Something about loving it or loving me, I don't know which. I've got my tongue in licking my own spunk. I'm going to eat Dr. Dave's ass too, make Rudy watch.

Tom fixes us a midnight snack, fruit, cheese and crackers. More wine. We always do this, food between us when we reek of sex. He's the opposite of Rudy, taller than me, bigger, solid, hairy. Blue collar rough to Rudy's pristine. "What are you thinking?" Tom asks. I take a bite of cracker, then a sip of wine, before I assure him my thoughts are his. "How happy I am," I tell him. He smiles and reaches over to tousle my hair.

"You know I love you, Nick," he says. "I can't help it. I respect your situation, but we're so good together. Aren't we good together?"

"We're wonderful together. Absolutely. And I adore you, Tom."

"I wish I could see you more than once a week."

"Now, come on, you said you respect things. I don't take a twelve year relationship lightly."

He goes quiet, curling his lips to hold back more words. I'm grateful for this as I don't want a scene. I take a piece of cheese and slide it to his mouth. He opens, licks my finger, and all is right again. Before leaving, I fuck him with the wine bottle.

Tuesday night Rudy shows me the new crown. "Last one." He sounds proud. Or maybe he thinks his mouth is worth a fortune, which is what's been spent.

"It's beautiful and I'm so happy for you." I kiss him.

Later, over drinks. out of the blue, he says, "Things are set for Saturday."

"Dr. Dave?"

"He'll be here at seven. After dinner."

I can't help but chuckle, and almost tip my glass and spill Pinot Noir. "Almost makes me want to skip date night."

"Me too! I'm glad you said that because I've been thinking the same thing. We should cancel our dates. I want to be sex-starved on Saturday."

Tom takes the cancellation well because it seldom occurs. I tell him we're going out of town, lie that Rudy's favorite aunt is in failing health. He buys this, offers hope she recovers quickly, and that we're not too upset. Tom's too bighearted for his own good. Skip is more suspect, probably because Rudy's not good with untruth. I don't get that. Lying is so easy. It feels smooth to me, sliding from my lips. I can almost taste it when I lie.

"We're all set then," I say when informed Rudy has managed the cancellation. We go to a movie Friday night to occupy ourselves and when we get home we don't have sex like usual. Nothing is said. We're both enjoying anticipation.

How does one prepare for a threesome? Deciding what to wear is uppermost, first impressions and all. We choose robes and nothing more. We set wine out to breathe and there's always liquor in case Dr. Dave requires it. "I want to call him Dr. Dave as we fuck," I say to Rudy as we wait on the doctor.

"I want to open my mouth and have him put is dick into it," Rudy replies. "God, how often I've thought of that while in the chair with my mouth full of instruments."

When the good doctor arrives we answer the door together, Rudy in his blue terry robe, me in my maroon, both chosen to enhance our coloring. Dave stuns us in jeans and loose fitting white shirt. We've only seen him in his blue doctor jacket, all prim and proper. Now we're treated to chest hair at the open collar and the white shirt makes him absolutely shine.

Dave Malone is a man of plenty, everything about him the ideal, including perfect white teeth. Somehow I know no work has been needed. He's brought wine and as I open it he slips out of his shirt like a guest shedding his coat. I steal glances as I pour the wine, pausing when his chest is bare because I'm lost in his fur and nicely rounded pecs. He catches me, smiles, and I fill the last glass.

"To us," he declares and we clink glasses which seems to be the official start of our endeavor. We take a good swallow, set aside the drinks, and as Dave strips we drop our robes. I glance at Rudy who holds his hard little cock like a kid needing to pee. I adore this look and usually dive down to suck him off, but not this time. I'm halfway along, as is Dave who presents the kind of cock given to a select few. I'm guessing eight, maybe nine inches which, considering his other attributes, seems fitting. I can't wait to get it inside me while I fuck Rudy.

Dave pulls both of us to him, but it's me he kisses. His tongue is eager and I hump his leg as I feast on him while his left hand is busy with Rudy. I reach for Dave's cock only to find a hand on it. Then Dave pulls back. "Bed?" he asks.

We run down the hall, pulling him along. Rudy leaps onto the bed and raises his legs to present his pink little pucker. "Somebody fuck me!" he cries.

Dave grabs a condom from the bedside stash, suits up, lubes himself, and spears my partner like I'm not in the room. Rudy lets out a familiar squeal as Dave starts a rhythmic thrust while I stand ignored at the bedside. Am I expected to just jump in? Will Dave accept that? Even if he does, the mechanics are off because there's no way I can manage a fuck train with him doing Rudy this way. I compromise and ease onto the bed, slide up beside them, and get a hand on Dr. Dave's ass. When he doesn't object I start to knead while savoring the feel of him fucking. He pauses his thrusting to push back at me so I wet a finger and, keeping to his resumed stroke, drive it into him. He issues a groan of welcome. Meanwhile, Rudy is babbling, then shrieking and coming which causes Dave to pick up his pace. I keep my finger in him and as he lets go his ass muscle clamps down. I stay inside him until he pulls out of Rudy. He then swings around and kisses me like before, tongue voracious. Like he never fucked Rudy at all.

Dave gets a hand on my dick and works me a little before dropping down to lie on his side and suck me. I'm totally gone on this until I see Rudy get in behind Dave and start to explore his ass. It occurs to me at this point that we have a train going now, just not the one I'd envisioned. Still, we have all night.

I'm swimming in pleasure with Dave's tongue working my dick and I want to keep him inside me so I try to hold off my climax. Every time I feel the stir, I think of drought, of parched ground and dead trees. This is always my go-to on those rare times I want to hold back and it works now. Dave isn't fazed by my lack of delivery and I like him being eager for a long feed.

Rudy now has his face buried in Dave's ass and I hear moaning and slurping which raises a thread of concern because he won't do this for me. I've eaten him out to excess because it drives him wild, but he's always said he'd throw up if he put his tongue in there. Now he's going at it and I don't hear any retching. Then Dave takes my nuts in hand and starts to work me, urging me toward a payoff so I concentrate on him, my dick in this gorgeous man's mouth, and suddenly I'm shooting and he's swallowing and all's right with the world.

As we wind down, Dave gives my softy a long suck, then pulls off. He also disengages from Rudy and goes to wash up while Rudy insists on kissing me. I want to say I'll throw up, but instead I allow the filthy tongue to caress mine because Dave's in there, even if once removed. When the good doctor settles back onto the bed, Rudy breaks from me to kiss him. There ensues a sort of writhing pile of flesh which I find I like, squirming, rubbing, tugging whatever is at hand. Sweat is plentiful as are fluids and soft moans. It's the epitome of wallow.

"I want a fuck train," I say from the pile. Cocks are up again and I reach over and grab a condom.

"Outstanding," offers Dave and he rises to suit up. Rudy, being a total bottom, watches. Maneuvering then begins and as Dave deftly places himself in the middle, he says, "Fuck me, Nick. Fuck me while I fuck Rudy. Fucking fuck train."

I want to say no, it's all wrong. I want to change the order, redirect things, complain, but I do as told, waiting while Rudy flips over to present his ass which Dave spears. "Come on, Nick," he urges when I pause. "Fuck my ass."

I crawl up behind him and slip my dick in which I tell myself isn't a bad second choice. When he starts to thrust into Rudy, I thrust accordingly, holding him at the hips as I ride the fuck train.

"I'm getting you both," Rudy calls. "Two guys fucking me at once. Oh God, fuck the hell out of me."

Dave doesn't say a thing. He keeps a steady stroke, just like the first time, and while I'm thrilled to be fucking this hot guy, I can't help but note this is twice for him doing Rudy. To chase off concern I look down at my cock driving into Dr. Dave and all else is forgotten. I grab his hips and begin to slam into him which all too quickly brings on a climax. Grunting and growling, I go at him until I go soft, then slip out and toss the rubber. I'm left to watch Dave fuck my partner for the second time, a fact which presents an undeniable truth. This is what Dave wants, who he wants. It was his idea, after all, the threesome. Did he engineer it so he could fuck Rudy without guilt? I mean, if you involve the partner you can do all you want and nobody can call it wrong. I sit back, having no desire now to do anything to Dave as he continues to fuck Rudy who's gone quiet. Images rush to mind, lurid pictures I cannot wipe away. I see the dental office, treatment room door closed, Dr. Dave in the chair, Rudy impaled on his cock. How long has it been going on? Are they in love or lust? I ease down beside them, watch Dave's cock go in and out of Rudy. He pulls back to let it ride up between Rudy's cheeks and grins at me. Here's a treat, it says, before he goes back in. In response I get a hand under Rudy and start milking his cock. Dave takes no further notice of me. Eyes closed, he continues to thrust until at last he groans and slams it home. Rudy, in response to my tugging, cries out and issues a few spurts.

This time we all wash up and Rudy dons a pair of shorts, saying, "I'm so full of come it'll be running out of me all night and I don't want it soiling anything."

"Let's have some wine," says Dave and he heads for the living room without waiting for comment. We take up abandoned glasses and Dave tops them off, then proceeds to drink half of his before sprawling on the couch. "So what now, boys? Is this just an evening thing or do I stay over? Up to you." He rubs his dick to help us decide.

"Oh, stay, stay," says Rudy without even a look my way. It's Dave who asks. "Nick?"

"Sure, yes, of course. Stay over."

It's not what I want, not at all, but how can I say no when Rudy is so eager? I want to take him aside and ask just what in hell is going on, but I have nothing coherent. Just this feeling that I'm being played. I slouch into an overstuffed chair while Rudy kneels beside Dave, attempting to look subdued when he's totally into this man. He takes a drink of wine, sets aside his glass, and proceeds to suck Dave's cock.

Rage ambushes me. A fire has begun in those drought-parched trees and swept into the house. I take large swallows of Merlot, attempting to cool down, but they have no effect. I suck in long breaths, all without notice by the others because Dave has his eyes closed and Rudy his mouth full. I could leave the room, but no, that's what they want. I attempt reason amid the conflagration, but am consumed by the fire. Finally I act. I get up, take the wine bottle in hand, then get in behind Rudy, wet a finger and shove it up his ass. He murmurs approval so I work him some, then, in one swift motion, withdraw the finger and shove the bottle neck up him.

"Ow!" he cries, pulling off Dr. Dave. "Hey, what are you doing?"

"Fucking you, my love. Giving you the fuck you deserve." My free hand has hold of his hip, my grip iron. I ram the bottle in a good dozen times before letting go. As it falls, I flee the scene. I throw on some clothes and when I pass the lovers on my return Dave is standing limp dicked and Rudy has the bottle in hand. "Nick," he says as I pass and that tears it because it's a dutiful Nick. In the car I slam it into gear and screech away. Let them have each other. Let them have it all, fuck the whole damned night.

I drive to Tom who I find clad in just blue boxers, television on to a reality show where everyone is naked in a singles bar. When I see him I burst into tears. He pulls me to him and says nothing, knowing, I suppose, that I'll spill soon enough. He holds me until I settle, then guides me to his couch, a roomy old thing he's had for years. We sink into it, my head on his shoulder, and he listens as I describe the threesome. "It sounded so good before, both of us thinking Dave was so hot. Sharing him like that made taking it up a step seem okay."

"That's a pretty big step," offers Tom. I sigh in agreement. His dog Rufus wanders in and comes over. He's a friendly sort, and he knows me. He's fourteen, golden retriever gone gray. I pet him, rub his neck, and he leans into me which makes me start crying again. When I finally stop, Rufus lies down at my feet.

"He's worried about you," says Tom.

"Good dog," I reply. I lean forward to pet him and Tom starts rubbing my back, petting me which is so warming I almost start blubbering again. "I'm not cut out for a threesome," I tell him. "I can have a partner and a boyfriend, but you get a crowd, well, now I know."

"How was the sex?" asks Tom.

"Great, only it didn't go like I thought. That was my mistake, figuring I'd get my way."

"What's your way?"

I chuckle, feeling embarrassed. "Why am I embarrassed?"

"No idea. You can do or say anything in here."

"I wanted a fuck train, me in the middle."

"And?"

"I ended up the caboose."

"So Dave fucked Rudy?"

"Twice. However we lined up or piled up or stretched out, it came out like that and finally, after all we'd done and Rudy started sucking Dave's dick, I lost it."

Tom pulls me back to him, slides an arm around me, and I sink into his world. We're quiet so long Rufus curls up and goes to sleep.

"How long for you and Rudy?" Tom asks. "I forget."

"Twelve years and he's even talked marriage."

"That surprises me, what with you each having somebody on the side."

"Me too. Christ, I don't know where I am."

"Right here." He kisses my cheek and I turn, find his mouth. How can I be hungry after the evening I've had? It's insane, but I'm suddenly voracious. Minutes later we're naked in bed and minutes more my legs are up on his shoulders as I take his formidable cock. "This is all you need," he says as he goes at me. His cock is thick and I groan as I take it while pumping my own in pure frenzy.

Tom grins when I unload, proud he's driven fresh spunk out of me. He then gets serious. His lips go up into a snarl and he starts to ream me until he's got my feet in his hands and is absolutely plowing me. I savor his grunts and growls as well as receiving his spunk.

He doesn't quit until he softens and once he slips out, he lowers my legs and crawls atop me. He lays his head next to mine, breathing hard, and I pat his back as I unwind from it all, the sex, the threesome, my life. Maybe some things are better left in twos. I want to tell him this, but for now quiet is best.

FANCY DRESS
CHRIS COLBY

The three of us had settled in well enough. Sharing a dorm with strangers was unusual but not altogether terrible. Being forced to at short notice, however, wasn't the ideal start. My friend James had ditched me at the last minute for a tiny off-campus bedsit that within a few weeks he was starting to regret, feeling he was missing out on "the full university experience". Despite my roommates still being mostly strangers to me, I did have to admit that it was nice to be able to come home to the sounds of other people.

Reggie was a big, broad-shouldered guy, the kind of person you expected to be the life of the party but in fact was very quiet, to the point that conversations with him could border on awkward. Living in such close proximity to him, I could see that he was incredibly shy but others didn't realise this, mistaking it for aloofness, especially since all of his friends were obnoxious engineering students who swaggered around Brunel University like reigning, vengeful gods. Those studying Arts, like myself, were at best mere mortals. Thankfully, Reggie never had his friends over to our dorm. He spent most of his time outside of his room quietly cooking intoxicating, rustic meals that filled our tiny kitchen with the heady aroma of herbs and spices, of garlic, of coriander, where everything was cooked from scratch and to perfection. It was hard to align the shy cook with his insufferable friends but being all of eighteen, I judged him by the people he hung out with and then forgot all about him.

So did our other flatmate, Graham. He was lean and tall, with a beautiful, angular face that looked permanently irritated. He moved across a room like he was cutting his way through. His clothes always accentuated his body; t-shirts a size too small that exposed his midriff, jeans slung low enough that you could easily sketch what was beneath them, sweats that stuck to him. I thought about doing things with him—to him—all the time. In my imagination, I walked up to him and demanded what I wanted, then and there. In reality, I stuttered and said nothing. Too busy daydreaming, I didn't realise that I actually knew very little about him. To this day, I'm still not entirely sure what he was studying.

The three of us spent most of our time alone in our rooms. This was not how I thought uni was going to be. I had told them both, the night we moved in, when politeness forced the three of us to get to know each other, that I was gay. Neither batted an eye—Graham didn't even look up from his phone—and I was utterly deflated. I had left my tiny village to come here, somewhere I could be myself, be gay and finally have all of those experiences I'd only read about and my announcement didn't even raise an eyebrow. Of course, when I thought about it, that's what I wanted, or at least what I thought I did. What I actually wanted was them to look at me a little differently, to see me as something a little more interesting for a moment.

Too cool for such a conversation, Graham was also gay but didn't tell us, leaving us to deduce this from his constant telephone arguments with his boyfriend Rupert. Graham spent almost all of his time in his room, on his mobile. Most of the conversations we heard through our paper-thin walls were of him, very slowly and over a number of concurrent arguments, breaking up with Rupert. Both Reggie and I had tried to get to know him a little and had offered him to join one or both of us in the kitchen on the rare times he briefly shared it but he just smiled no, pointed at his phone call in progress as if it was something entirely out of his hands, and left.

"It's the way you say the name *Rupert*. *Rupert*," my friend Simon said. During lunch, he insisted that I had a thing for Graham. I had said that he was cute and a nice guy but that I didn't *like* him, and that I just didn't like the way that *Rupert*…and then I heard the inflection in my voice, and I realised that maybe I *did* have a thing for him. Of course, as soon as I realised this, I found it impossible to be around him. Such occurrences were rare but Graham's voice always echoed around his room, somehow piercing beyond it, like he was everywhere. That night, the wall between us seemed especially thin; he spent most of his evening on his mobile, bitching with his friends about Rupert but I felt like he was talking directly to me.

A couple of days after lunch with Simon, my friend Alastair decided to take matters in hand. "Look, babe, no one cares about this breakup except for you. I haven't even met Graham." He narrowed his gaze and gestured at the scrap of paper in front of me. "Write down your suggestion already."

Alistair, Simon, and Simon's friend Claude and I had decided we were going to dress up for Halloween. We had been debating for weeks what to go as and our group suggestions were inevitably shot down by one or more of the group— The Fantastic Four, The Beatles, The A-Team—so instead, with Halloween looming, we decided to each write down one idea and put them in a hat. The only rule was that the costumes had to be simple and easily sourced. Whoever had the best costume got drinks bought for them by the others all night. I wrote down *cowboy* and stuck it in the hat.

Simon, jumping at the chance for a little pomp and circumstance, shook the hat as if he were auditioning for *All That Jazz*. We were not a receptive audience. Alastair went first and got *superhero* and Simon got my *cowboy*. I reached my hand in and read the slip aloud.

"Drag? Who put this in? The costume is supposed to be simple."

Claude smiled. "But it is simple, Brian. All you need is a dress and a wig."

I exhaled loudly. Claude smiled wider. "Sure, it should be no problem for you. Being gay and all."

"Let's hope the last one says dickhead. You won't need a costume." As he reached in, I muttered a little prayer that one of the others *had* put in something complicated.

Claude's face dropped. "The Incredible Hulk? You're taking the piss. That's going to be way too hard to do."

"Seems simple enough to me Claude—just some green body paint. Unless you want to swap and you can do drag? I hear lots of straight boys like to be able to dress up in drag on Halloween. Kinda like a gateway drug."

"Fuck off, Brian."

I giggled under my breath. I had gotten off easy.

⚜

I HEARD HIM before I even got in the door.

Rupert, listen, we can make this work if you want to make this work. I'll be home for Christmas, and—well if you don't want to—Rupert, you're being ridiculous. We can make this work if you want to. If you want to break up…well…we can do that too. I just, you need to work out what you want Rupert…Well, why did you go to Manchester then?

I hadn't really paid attention to any of his conversations in a while. It was easy to forget that theirs was a real relationship, so familiar were Graham's constant monologues but for the first time in a long time, I realised that they were much more to him than the background noise it was to me and Reggie. I could hear the pain in his voice. My mind wandered to how I could help, how I'd take care of him. I imagined being his shoulder to cry on, the person he turned to. I imagined that after a while he'd look at me the way I stole looks at him. I fantasised that his hands were all over me, his cock hard and pressed against me, his lips exploring—

The sound of glass breaking and a muffled *Fuck!* coming from the kitchen.

After dumping my bag in my room, I headed to the kitchen to investigate, as well as to see what I could scavenge. Reggie was cooking bolognese. It smelt wonderful. He had broken a glass but by the time I said hi, he had cleaned it up and just nodded back, busy again in the rhythm of cooking. Searching through the cupboards, all I found was a small tin of spaghetti hoops and some bread. Suddenly, I wasn't that hungry—certainly not enough to make it alongside Mr. Culinary. I returned to my room and started studying.

About ten minutes later, there was a knock at my door. Reggie, wearing a spattered apron, offered me dinner. "If you want some, I made way too much. I'm just going to serve it up now. Uh, you hungry?"

I should've said yes, and joined him but for a moment, I thought that he pitied me so instead I politely declined. He looked disappointed, forced a smile and left.

As soon as I closed the door, I realised he was probably just being nice. In all the time we'd lived together, he'd never offered me to join him for dinner before, and now that he had, I'd said no. By the time I decided to go join him, the kitchen was empty and I couldn't work up the courage to knock on his door.

※

I HAD FALLEN asleep reading about Vikings. I dreamt of Reggie as a Viking warrior, eating something roasted, swigging from a tankard and talking to me about where we were going next. His thick dirty hair was so long it hit his shoulders. His sword was propped up beside him. He was talking about strategy and revenge. He was so handsome it floored me. After a few minutes, he realised I wasn't listening. He jumped up, reached around and grabbed my hair, pulling my head back. He smiled and said, "You're listening now, aren't you, Balder?" and he roughly stroked the side of my face with his knuckles. He leaned in closer, his lips open and I was jolted awake by a knock at the door.

Half-asleep, I thought it might be Reggie. In case it wasn't, I threw on a pair of sweats to conceal my hard-on, still hoping for the dream to continue, despite the voice in my head insisting, *you've never ever thought of him like that before.* I opened the door. Graham was leaning against the doorframe.

"Can I come in?" His eyes were heavy with sex. He had been drinking; drunk to the point of stumbling a little but still upright and retaining his charm. The smell of whiskey on his breath floated into the room.

"Uh." My cock remained hard but my brain panicked and shut down completely. You're on your own with this one, mate. He took a swig from the bottle he'd been holding. Here he was: the guy from the other side of the wall that I'd been fantasising about for months. I had no idea what to do. "Did you have a good night, Graham?"

"Not really."

He didn't say anything else. He just stood there, staring at me, waiting for me to invite him in. As he waited comfortably in the silence, he took another, longer swig from his bottle, wiping his mouth with the back of his hand. This wasn't a Graham I recognised.

"Did something happen? Is everything okay with Rupert?"

As soon as I said his name, everything changed. Still hard, I realised that I should've asked him in, kissed him, spent the night doing everything every which way, but now it was too late. When he heard his boyfriend's name, all possibility of me and him doing anything tonight drained away. He slumped against the door.

"Do you want to come in and talk?"

Graham sighed. He stared at the bottle of whiskey.. "Nah, another time. Sorry for bothering you man. G'night." He went into his room and closed the door.

He wasn't bothering me. How long had I been wanting him to do exactly what he had done? And now I'd messed it up. I looked at myself in the mirror and told myself, probably loud enough for the entire flat to hear, that I was a fucking idiot.

⚜

BY THE TIME I got up the next day, the flat was empty. I checked my phone—there was a text from Claude, with a photograph of him starting to apply the green body paint. It read, *better bring your wallet.*

No way was I letting him win. Not a chance.

I texted my friend Lori and told her that I was doing drag for Halloween and that I needed her help. I was going to text her again to see if she wanted me to bring anything but before I could she texted back, all in caps, telling me that she had the perfect dress, and to be at hers after class. Lori loved projects, especially ones where she got to open her giant, steel makeup box which was the size of a large footstool. Before I could put my phone in my pocket, she had texted again. *Don't forget to shave. All. Over.*

By the time I'd done that and showered, I was almost late and had to rush to get over to her, just catching her heading into her building. I handed her the bottle of vodka I had brought as a thank you and she bellowed dramatically, "Let's begin!"

She dumped the vodka, brought out the make-up and told me to sit. She squinted at me, like a painter framing a portrait in his mind and giggled to herself. She dug into her makeup box and started plucking out some essentials.

"This is going to be *brilliant*. Trust me." She opened the vodka and handed me an empty tumbler. Half an hour in, I was mildly drunk and couldn't see much of a difference. She flitted around me, telling me to stay still, and that "It's going on your eyes, not in them, would you relax!"

Finally, she took the vodka and handed me a mirror. She had utterly transformed me. I didn't recognise myself—the entire shape of my face had changed. I said as much, and as she got stuck into the vodka, she said "Men think it's a chore but makeup is amazing."

As we drained the bottle, she got more and more excited as the look came together.

"—Oh, and these shoes!—No, wait, with *this* wig!—you *have* to wear a *bra!*—"

Finally, she put her hands over my eyes and moved me towards the mirror. When she took them away and went "Ta-Da", I thought I was going to laugh but I looked...*beautiful*. Kitted out in a floor length black number, with a wig that looked more real than her hair and makeup worthy of a magazine, I stuttered and stumbled over my words. She poured herself another vodka and beamed at me like a proud mother. I thanked her profusely, and she ordered takeout to line my stomach. I daintily ate it as she did her own makeup in a flash—she was going up the town, somewhere with her current boyfriend. Finally, she took ten or fifteen pictures of me, "for blackmail purposes later" she said, and sent me on my way.

Claude looked a mess. His arms were streaked with lime green body paint. He looked like he'd been attacked by a class full of hyperactive children that had just been taught how to finger-paint. He had ripped a shirt of his and drawn on some exaggerated chest muscles in what looked like—but I hoped for his sake wasn't—black permanent marker. He looked at me and his mouth hung open. Immediately, Alastair and Simon said, "Okay, you definitely win" and Claude's mouth clenched shut.

The night was a haze of alcohol; every time my glass was empty, another drink appeared, and not just from Alastair and Simon—I had lots of male attention from cute, half-cut straight boys, a couple of whom I was convinced actually thought I was a girl. Claude spent most of the night nursing a pint and sulking on the couch in the corner. When he got up to finally get another drink, security saw the green streak marks all over the furniture and asked him to leave. According to Alastair and Simon, he told them to fuck off. By the time they grabbed him by the arms, Claude was screaming bloody murder and threatening the bouncers personally, who after that literally threw him out onto the pavement. All this had to be explained to me later; I'd been dirty dancing with a cute boy dressed as Superman and missed the entire thing.

Warmed by some whiskey, I walked home without as much as a jacket, tottering down the road in my heels, giggling to myself. I got home and threw out a loud "Hello?" to see if anyone was around. Silence. I downed nearly a pint of water, dehydrated from the packed club. I dropped the glass in the sink and turned to stumble to my room, and was startled to find Reggie staring at me from the doorway.

My feet, barely stuffed into Lori's heels, were now killing me. I kicked them off and smiled at Reggie. "Hey man, have a good night?"

He didn't speak. He was breathing heavily but he didn't move, his expression was unreadable. He could have been happy, or bored, or annoyed, or having a stroke for all I could tell. Having never seen him drunk before, I figured this must be what he looked like when he was.

"Well, I hope you did. I had a great night. But now, I need to get the hell out of this," I said, gesturing to the drag.

Still no response. Shrugging my shoulders, I muttered "okay" and went to the bathroom. Catching sight of myself in the mirror, I realised I was a little drunker than I thought I was. My makeup was smeared and I was glad that it was time to get out of it. I stripped and washed my face, all of the makeup falling away, leaving only the bits that Lori been warned would require her specialist 'tools' and I spent almost half an hour enjoyably scrubbing the night off in a piping hot shower.

I threw on a t-shirt and a pair of boxers and headed to the kitchen to make something to eat. Reggie was sitting at the kitchen table; I don't think he'd left.

"I had a good night, thanks," he said, finishing our conversation from earlier, as if I'd just asked him.

I laughed. He bunched his eyebrows as he tried to talk. "Sorry, you, I didn't expect to…I was surprised." Embarrassed, he stared at the floor.

I started rooting through the cupboards. "Alastair and the others. We decided to dress up, pick suggestions from a hat. Claude stuck it in, trying to be funny but I ended up winning best costume and getting drinks bought for me all night."

He looked at me directly, his eyes holding my gaze. "I'm not surprised. You looked fucking hot."

All notion of what I came into the kitchen for fell away. "What?"

"You looked fucking hot." Then he exhaled the effort it took for him to say that.

"I'm not a girl, that was just…I'm not into –".

The hard bit done, he relaxed and smiled widely. "I know." He stood up and came towards me.

As he approached me, I remember thinking, *you've never had this, ever, someone likes you, wants you, and this is how it feels, they've put themselves out there and you get to respond, you have the next move.* For a second I felt like I was back in the dream from the day before. Until he touched me, his hand on my chest, moving down to my forearm, his hand on my bare skin.

My body was lost in feeling. My brain scrambled to catch up. "I thought you were straight."

His body against mine, his hands were a blur all over me, his cock hard against me.

A smirk. "Shut up, Brian."

He pulled my t-shirt over my head and flung it behind him, his tongue working its way down my chest. My cock hardened and sprung from my boxers and he pulled them all the way down. Kneeling in front of me, he stared at my dick. He leaned back and looked me over, his eyes working their way back down to my crotch. He bit his lip and slowly inched towards it. Stopping just short of my cock, he smiled, before leaning forward and swallowing it, taking the length of it effortlessly. He withdrew, catching his breath, and licked the spit from his lips.

He devoured me again, building up a rhythm. My mind was blank; I was unable to speak. It was only when he stopped that I realised my eyes were closed, and when I opened them he was there, his mouth on my neck, his lips finding mine, his hand at the back of my head, pulling me closer.

My hands pulled at his clothes, pushing his t-shirt up to his chest, pulling open his jeans. As he pried off the tee, I opened his belt and shoved my hand down his pants. He groaned when I gripped him, as if it hurt, but it was the surprise of my touch that pushed him forward, breathless, his face pressed into my chest. He opened his jeans completely and let them fall to the floor. Unconstrained, he bit one nipple and pinched the other. He grew harder in my hand as I wanked him.

I lifted him up for a kiss, and saw something out of the corner of my eye.

Graham stood in the doorway, staring at us. I think he had been there for some time. He looked ready to pounce but when I met his eyes they were full of hurt, that said *You brushed me off, and now you're with him.*

I froze. I'd wanted him for so long and the way he was looking at me, it felt like it would never happen now.

Reggie put a hand on my shoulder. He had seen Graham, and now he was looking at me, waiting for my reaction. Was Reggie a little hurt too? The lust drained out of me and suddenly I felt very cold. I was about to move, to stop, to say that I was going to my room and not coming out for the rest of the year, when Reggie, still staring at me, looked at Graham and with a slight movement of his head beckoned him over.

Reggie dropped to his knees and started licking my cock, teasing the head with his tongue as Graham came towards me. He stopped in front of me, unsure, and I reached out and brought him closer. My breath was heavy with him being so close to me and he saw this. He ran his hand across my nipple experimentally and I felt like I would melt. He smiled and started to kiss my chest, my neck. His tongue plunged deep inside my mouth as Reggie took my cock completely. I closed my eyes and in the dark, mouths moved around my body, tongues explored every crevice, every hole, lips wet against my chest, my mouth, my asshole. I opened my eyes and watched them move around me, unable to speak. I was the centre of the universe. They didn't ignore each other, as much as focus completely on me, licking, stroking, pulling, gripping, twisting, sucking, and probing everywhere.

When I opened my eyes, Graham had stripped down to a jockstrap. I wanted to remove that last scrap of fabric and bury my head within. Reggie was behind me, arm around me, pulling me back, biting my neck whilst Graham was on his knees, spread low and wide, his tongue out as I slapped my cock off it, one hand of his gripping my balls, the other working his nipples.

I moved Reggie around and signalled Graham up. They stood patiently in front of me, curious at what I would do. I kissed Reggie, gentle at first, then urgently, ferociously before pulling back. The momentum of the kiss had him stumble forward into the empty space. He looked mildly high, perfectly relaxed, and satiated. I could clearly see the way he looked at me now, and whilst I didn't share it the same way, I wanted this, I wanted him now and I was glad that he had started it.

With my hand still trailing over Reggie, I kissed Graham the same way. Somewhere in the back of my brain, the rational part of me was astounded at my confidence, but that was soon forgotten. There was nothing but Graham's mouth, his hands, his body against my skin, hot to the touch and seemingly everywhere at once. As the kiss grew deeper and longer, I pulled Reggie towards us.

Then I moved away, and pushed them closer. They looked at each other quizzically. I nodded yes, please, bit my lip and leaned back against the counter watching Reggie and Graham kiss. They laughed slightly, at the oddness of it; two men who had never fancied each other, but here they were, cocks hard, breathless and tongues entangled as I watched, stroking myself. Their tongues thrust deeper as my cock grew harder. After a couple of minutes, they stopped. Reggie lightly slapped the side of Graham's face in blokish solidarity and Graham laughed.

They turned to face me and the laughter died away. With a look to Reggie, Graham pulled me towards him and bent me over. Reggie guided my head towards his cock and began to facefuck me. Gripping my hair, he thrust in and out of my mouth, slowly at first. With each thrust, he went deeper and harder. I could feel my gag reflex tickling at the back of my throat but I breathed deeply through my nose to suppress it, and as he continued to fuck my mouth, the fresh air was drowned out by the heady scent of his crotch, all sweat and musk. I was lost in his motion until I felt cold liquid being worked into my ass. Graham found my hand and brought it to his now sheathed and lubed cock, letting me know that he was safe and ready. I fingered my hole briefly as guidance and as soon I pulled my fingers away, he slid inside me.

And you thought it would be awkward handjobs with drunk straight boys forever...

Once Graham was in, neither of them showed me any mercy. They fucked me like animals, thrusting themselves inside me, as I moaned. Neither wanted to switch, they were content to fuck me from the ends they had me. Time became meaningless, I was a mouth getting fucked, an ass getting rammed, flesh getting pulled and stroked by hands eager for somewhere to anchor, holes being filled with friction. My body was slack and pliable between them. My hands were down by my side, not daring to touch my cock, steadily dripping pre-cum. I didn't want to come, not yet.

They were pounding me now, grunting and moaning, cheering me on whilst all I could express around the cock in my mouth were guttural consonants. Then a chance to draw a breath; Reggie pulled out from my mouth, globs of my spit trailing after his cock. He gripped and jerked it and grabbed my face roughly. "Stick out your tongue." I did as I was told. I would've done so anyway. "D'you want my cum? You gonna take it? Are you, gonna—"

He knelt on the floor and leaned back. Graham pushed us down to Reggie's level. Slightly arched, with his knees under him, Graham went even deeper. I moaned loudly and involuntarily. Reggie watched me moan and growled, "Fuck, yeah". He pulled my face towards his cock and with a scream started to come. Graham leaned forward, pushing me onto Reggie's cock, until I gagged. I felt a hot load spurt down my throat.

Reggie pulled his dick free and lay backwards, gasping for breath. I felt Graham withdraw. With a scream, he shot his load all over my asshole.

I lay down on the floor, trying and failing to catch my breath. Reggie bent down, his tongue darting around my aching cockhead. Graham pushed my legs in the air and started licking his cum from my asshole. Reggie sucked me faster and faster, Graham pushed his tongue inside my hole and I came writhing and shouting, as if I were having a fit.

If this is what coming was, if this was what *sex* was, I had never had it before tonight.

We fell to the floor in whatever positions we were in, unable to move. My breathing slowed and the room slowly started to come back into focus.

One of them snickered and said, "Happy Halloween."

❦

AT SOME POINT, we all went back to our own beds. The next morning, Reggie was cooking a fry-up and we all came together for breakfast. We talked, not about the night before (although there were still smiles all round), but about everything else, about where we came from, about our courses, our families. That morning, we became friends. We never had sex again.

Graham asked over breakfast if we were the first people he had come out to. Reggie nodded.

Reggie said, "Well, I didn't really come out."

Graham moved closer and whispered conspiratorially, "If it helps, I'm gay too".

I pushed him in the shoulder, "Yeah, we'd worked that one out."

He pushed me back, saying, "Well, at least I didn't have to make a big *announcement* about it the first night we met."

Reggie crunched his way through slice of toast, "Yeah, Brian, that was really lame."

I jokingly swore at them, mock-offended, and we happily ate our breakfast, basking in the afterglow of the night before.

THE GUARDS OF GOVERNOR'S SQUARE

SHANE ALLISON

I stuck the last orange and hot-pink flyer on the windshield of some piece of shit Ford Tempo. Sweat cascaded down my back into the ditch of my ass, not to mention my glasses slip-and-sliding from behind my ears. My tee-shirt was soaked. The acid wash jeans stuck to the skin of my thighs and my bare feet slid around in the confines of my Rockports.

The cool air of the mall ran across my hot face as I entered through its advertisement-plastered glass double doors. I thought for sure I would die from thirst if there wasn't a water fountain or a Coke in my immediate future. I bought the biggest soda they had at Aunt Annie's. Temporarily sated, I decided to do a little cruising—see if there were any new sharks circling the waters.

The bathrooms were at the ass end of a spiralled hall that was cut off from the rest of the mall. The security and management office were the only two places that did business down that hidden, hollow corridor.

I had become a regular in the tearooms. So much so that a jeri-curl-haired janitor warned me that if I wasn't careful, I would get caught. But what the hell did he know? I had only been cruising for damn near four years. Had my eye on my own ass before I could watch anyone else's—was always cautious of the shit going down around me. I went from movie theatre urinals to blowing guys in neck-twisting positions beneath partitions. All that and never caught.

That was until this racist, homophobic, piece-of-shit, redneck toy cop threatened to arrest me weeks before.

He was onto me. I was getting sloppy, wasn't being as careful as I thought. I guess seeing my face four or five times in the same day—in the same toilet—planted a seed of suspicion.

"Yes, sir. Sorry, sir," I kept saying. The brute manhandled my person, practically dragging me by my shirt, out of the mall.

It was on a Sunday when the shit hit the fan.

I sat in the stall that day for a good two hours at least watching men through the slit of my stall door wash their hands, listening to fathers scold their sons about touching the dirty sinks. A few men stopped to glance my way as I put on a jack off show, but none were interested in partying seriously. The only way I could catch any action was if I stood and gawked over the wall of my stall. A lot of farting mostly—funny how those animal instincts kick into full gear when men think they're alone.

When I saw a cute blond walk across me to the vacant stall, it was a relief from the daddies trolling around. As he ducked in, I heard that familiar sound of a stall door being shut, a latch of metal being pushed closed.

I wasted no time in taking a peek, alert for the slightest movement that would give me a reason to think he was into other men. I tapped my foot to let him know that I was cool, watched religiously for his response. He slid his Asics slightly across the cold floor of tile—men like me know to signals to give, but it wasn't one I was familiar with.

After hours of sitting, my legs were starting to fall asleep. Wriggling to get more comfortable, I knocked over a roll of toilet paper that had been sitting on a small, metal banister screwed to the partition between us. It rolled under the trade's stall, touching his right foot. I snatched the roll off the floor and thrust it back in its precarious place.

"Sorry," I whispered.

There was a pause. Then:

"Not a problem," he told me.

After that split second of awkwardness, I tapped my Rockports to his attentions once more. This time he got it. He nudged me with the tip of his shoe.

I bent and bowed my body until my muscles burned in an attempt to see if he was doing something lewd and lascivious, but to no avail: all I witnessed were shoes, white tennis shorts and legs grown with hairs of honey gold. I figured *hell, if he tapped that foot, he's cool, right?* I had a while left before my bus was due, and I didn't want to miss my chance with this beefcake. He was too good to pass up—another tawdry entry for my journal.

I dropped to my knees, thrust my dick beneath the wall that separated us.

I didn't hear him move, there was no shuffling of shoes, no rustling of bunched clothing. I held my breath, hoping I would feel a hand or mouth—anything—touch my exposed cock.

"All right, I need you to stand up and step out of the stall," he said. His voice was stern and serious enough to kick-start my heart racing. I pushed myself off my knees and yanked my jeans up around my bare ass, fumbling to cover myself.

"Open the door and step out," he said, hammering against the wall of the cubicle.

I didn't have to act dumb, didn't have to guess what was going on. I was caught. I thought of that jeri-curl janitor who tried to warn me, and that redneck cop, the feel of his gritty mitts around my neck. This blond was no trick, but one of the mall security guards.

He grabbed my arm tight and escorted me out of the bathroom down the bare corridor to the security office with its peeling letters on smudged plate glass. He pointed to a blank white wall and told me to stand in front of it—in a voice that was taking no argument—and face him.

I did as I was told. Fear pumped through me, my pits dripping with sweat.

He opened one of the drawers of the desk and fished out a Polaroid camera. "Look at me," he said, and snapped a picture. Thirty seconds later, there I was: immortalized in my horrid, green tee.

He pointed to a metal chair pulled away from the desk. "Sit," he said, without looking at me.

He produced a carbonated form out of a paper stack. "Name and address?" he said. Unable to think fast enough to make something up, I gave him them both. My tongue felt thick in my mouth, and I was having trouble swallowing. He wrote down what I told him, head bent as he wrote slowly, pausing only to check the spelling of my street.

When he was done, he set the pen down and looked at me. "I'm Officer Sutter," he said. He explained that they were getting some complaints about men having sex in the bathrooms, men like me. I thought of this one old fuck in particular—I'd bet it was him had tipped them off. Probably just wanted the tearoom to himself.

"We're taking this very seriously," Sutter told me.

I wondered if jail was anything like those prison movies. Perish the thought of getting butt-fucked against my will.

Sutter took his walkie-talkie and spoke in that indecipherable kind of talk that only cops talk in. In amongst the string of code-words, he mentioned a name and it snagged at my memory: that day I was tossed out on my ear. It was him, the hick guard that had warned me with burning words still embedded in my brain. I saw his fat, round face, and the name metal pinned to his standard issue uniform. *Grisham*.

When he arrived, I looked away and stared at the side wall littered with JUST SAY NO posters and pics of those wanted for crimes of shoplifting. Grisham walked in big, breathing heavy and pig-like. Figures, I thought. His gut was tight under his uniform shirt, the straining belt glistening beneath the stark office lights. Sweat poured from his face, soaking the stiff collar of his shirt.

"Thought I told *you* to stay out of here?" he said.

There was a wedding band on his finger—a little too tight, the pudgy skin raw and red around it. I felt for his wife. This porker had to be at least three-hundred-and-fifty pounds. She'd be better married to someone like Sutter, who was built like a brick Texas shithouse with feathers of golden hair, fire-blue eyes and a face strewn with freckles. His ass was firm. His tennis shorts rode between the crack of his pert butt, and it hadn't gone unnoticed. Sutter's body was poetry in motion. I studied *his* hands for any signs of marriage, but there was none.

Grisham forced himself between us, obstructing my view with his fat ass. I looked him up and down and gave him the kiss off.

"I told you if you came back here, I would arrest your black ass." It felt like he wanted to say something else other than "black." His true colors was showing. With duress, he pulled my mug up to his own and said, "I'm talkin' to you, boy."

"Grish, take it easy," Sutter said. "Here's his ID.

Grisham squinted at it. "So where you live at, boy? Looks here like a Woodville address. Is that where you live, boy, out in the sticks? Didn't know they had niggers livin' out there."

"That's enough, Grish.." Sutter's tone was sharp. seemed He seemed more sympathetic to my plight.

"I tol' him what I would do to him if I caught his ass back in the shitters," said Grisham.

"We're not doing that. Remember what happened to the last guy we did that to?" Sutter grinned. Not a friendly grin.

"So whatchu wanna do with 'im?" I wondered just what the hell he meant. Now I was *really* scared shitless. I was terrified they would beat me to a pulp and toss me out with the food court trash.

"You wanna call it in?" Grisham said.

Sutter sighed. "They're just going to let him off with a summons to appear in court. I have a better idea."

They turned away from me, huddled in the corner, talking in low muttered voices that I couldn't hear. Every now and then, one or the other would glance over their shoulder to look at me. I thought about making a run for it, but figured the athletic Sutter would be on my ass before I could say *cinnabon*.

I hoped that whatever they were saying involved my being let go.

"Stand up and turn around," said Grisham.

I opened my mouth—

"Just do it," said Sutter.

I looked to the blond for signs of mercy in those eyes, but there was none.

"Now place your hands on your head and cross your fingers."

I felt like I was in some crazy fucking episode of *Cops*. The steel of the cuffs were cold as they were bound around my wrists. *Shit. Who can I call to bail me out? Linda? Marcus? Collin? Someone good for money…*

The brute pushed me closer to the wall. "And don't move."

My face kissed the cold bricks. Looking sidelong at the door, through the blinds that shrouded the plate glass a woman yapped away on a pay phone. She didn't look my direction. Behind me, I heard the rustle of movement. *What are they doing?* I tried to focus on their image reflected in the glass—were they *undressing* each other?

They were. Unfastening buttons, undoing polyester pants. The whole thing was freaky and gross, but I couldn't look away. Grisham was bear-chested with waves of brunette fur overlooking the neck of his tee-shirt, Sutter's hands tangling in the fur. *Am I in some morbid Stanley Kubrick movie?* How was it possible that this blond angel was into this sweaty, mammoth of a beast? Were these guys' even real cops or posers, lovers on the down-low? It would be the perfect set up. The only way they could see one another without drawing suspicion to themselves. Jesus!

Grisham dropped to his knees. He worked Sutter's dick out of the cotton panel of his underwear and began to stroke him. Sutter's uncut, corpulent cock curled up like a banana, the foreskin near covering the blond's entire head, leaving only the piss slit exposed.

My own dick hardened within its confines.

Was beginning to lose feeling in the right side of my hand, but I dared not complain out of fear that it would be the end of me. Had no other choice than to watch the plate glass scene of unadulterated fornication. Grisham was a typical porker with his wife beater tee and white boxers. He peeled Sutter's foreskin back and began to lap at the head of his dick. Sutter, with bent knees, and a freckled, unconcealed ass, raised his eyes to meet mine in the reflection as I stood there pressed to the wall.

Grisham went full force: stroke, suck, repeat. Grisham was loud. I was surprised at the way he went on. I expected that woman on the phone to look up and hear him through the wall. Sutter lifted the tail end of his shirt, exposing a ripped, tan torso, and thrusted, He fucked Grisham's fat face. The bigger man's balding skull bobbed and weaved in an attempt to keep up with his partner.

My own dick was twitching crazy in my pants aching for release. This was better than any cheap porn flick. I pressed myself against the wall—anything to put pressure on my hard-on.

"Turn around," Sutter commanded.

Sutter had pressed Grisham's head deep into his crotch, all of him disappeared into the guard's mouth. It was hard to believe the mutt was married considering the way he sucked a dick. Seeing the action in person was so much more of a thrill than watching it in smudged glass. I couldn't keep my eyes off Grisham, the way he kept at Sutter. I would have given anything to know what Sutter's dick was like wallowing around in my own mouth.

"Come here," he said. I practically ran.

Sutter reached for my zipper. I kept my eyes on his hands expertly opening my pants, somehow afraid that I would be turned to dust if I looked into those fiery blue eyes. He smelled of cigarettes; I breathed him in.

I was nowhere near as well-endowed as Sutter, but was proud of what I did have between these knees. It tickled as he crept up, pulling elastic over my hard on. I shut my eyes: darkness as I felt a dry palm around my dick. There was a tug and a jerk, and another, and another. I shut my eyes, tighter and tighter till it hurt. Ass and aftershave filled my lungs. There was that line of sweat cascading down my back again.

As Sutter took me, I thought of all those boys during my own boyhood: Von Ash's lips around my dick, Daniel Stewart's bucked teeth, John David referring to it as a boner.

And then there was a calm, sleek cool that overran me from below. I cracked my left eye to find Grisham bearing down on my dick. He had moved from Sutter's to mine—going back and forth in fact, from one hard dick to the other giving them both equal attention.

I opened my eyes wide and Grisham pulled me in close. He turned to Sutter's cock, but Sutter refused and pushed Grisham's face firmly back to me. Sutter ran his hand over my groin as Grisham blew, and pulled down my jeans further along to expose my butt.

Sutter reached behind, finger forcing itself between my cheeks and pushing into my hole. It hurt at first, but once he was well in, I took it like a trooper, savouring the feeling of his slim finger moving deep inside my body. I tightened myself, clamping tight around him, and he moaned and pulled me into kiss him.

Between my legs, Grisham sucked my dick head, and out of nowhere I was coming hard and sudden in the brute's mouth. He didn't swallow, simply reached up to the desk for a coffee cup and spit me into the bottom. I watched my seed mingle with the dregs and darken.

Sutter pushed me away, and with my hands still cuffed, I collapsed awkwardly into the chair, my spent dick hanging out of my zipper. His eyes never leaving mine, Sutter bent over the desk, exposing his pale ass to Grisham's grubby mitts. Grisham spread him eagerly, stuffing his thick fingers into his butt. I watched the gold ring thrust back and forth against the hole.

Sutter's hand was between his legs working his cock. His face turned redder than dawn, and he spattered thickly across the desk.

Grisham sank back on his fat haunches. His eyes were red and watery. There was a trace of me left at the corner of his mouth.

"What do you wanna do with 'im?" Grisham said, looking at me.

Sutter ran a finger through the cooling seed on the table, and stepped over to me. He tucked my dick back into my jeans and zipped me up. He turned me around and freed my hands from the steel binds. His finger ran across my lips, and I licked his finger clean—it filled my mouth, salty and strong. "A trespassing warning will be issued," he said quietly in my ear. "If you come back onto the premises of the mall, you *will* be arrested."

The whole bus ride home, I could still taste him on my tongue.

SPRING ON SCRABBLE CREEK

JEFF MANN

THE LOVERS JUMPED from here, they say. I stand near the edge of the ledge and look down into the gorge, over steep slopes, April-green treetops, and the curve of the New River hundreds of feet below. I can hear, just barely, the rumble of whitewater over rocks. Up this high, the breeze is cool and constant, mussing my hair and beard.

Lover's Leap, this place is called. There's some legend about a Native American couple who wanted to marry real bad but their families wouldn't allow it, so they ended up jumping off this bluff so they could be together in death—kinda like Appalachian Romeo and Juliet. That's a leap my lover Derek hasn't asked of me yet, but one day, who knows? I'm tired of aging, that's for sure. Derek doesn't know it, but lately I've been plucking goddamn gray hairs out of my eyebrows.

I'm scared of heights, so my palms are sweating by the time I move real careful away from the edge. I turn and take the steep steps back, looking for wildflowers in the woods —the botanists call 'em "spring ephemera"—as I head up the hill.

Here's a few now, growing up out of black-rot humus past springs have made. I bend to stroke the tender leaves and petals. Bluebells, just like the ones

I used to find along the Greenbrier River when I was a kid in Summers County. A couple of dog's-tooth violets. May apples, with their funny little umbrellas. Bloodroot: that white, white blossom, whiter'n any snow I've ever seen. If you were to dig, you'd find the root. If you break it, it bleeds, a red juice that'll coat your palms like some kinda evidence of a crime…or the aftermath of a hungry, sharp-toothed mouth. The red that smears my neck and nipples, my pecs and cock after Derek's done making love to me.

Well, that thought has me stiff in my shorts, and it is getting toward sunset. I wanna snuggle with my man before he wakes. I pluck a bloodroot blossom before picking up my pace and heading toward the lodge.

જે

BEST ROOM IN the house, as usual, the deluxe suite at Hawk's Nest State Park. Derek's collected quite a fortune in his long life, and, born in Scotland the way he was, he's got the same kind of clan-system mentality that we West Virginia boys have: kick your enemies' butts and take good care of your friends and kin. He's always spoiling me. Even after nearly eleven years together, I still ain't used to it. I sure do appreciate it, though.

The shades are drawn tight, and a Do Not Disturb sign has kept away any puttering maids. Derek's sprawled on his belly on the big bed, twisted up in a sheet. I put the bloodroot flower in a glass and set it on the bedside table, and then I sit on the edge of the bed, pull back the sheet, and watch my naked husbear sleep.

Goddamn, he's a glory. Tall, muscled, furry…the sex-demon of my dreams. Thank God I got over my initial fear and gave us a chance. I run my hand over his smooth back and down his spine. I pat his pale ass and stroke the black fur—soft as fern fronds—between his butt-cheeks. I squeeze his firm biceps, trace his tattoos, and run my fingers through his shaggy hair and bushy beard. His hair's so black. I can't help but hum a few bars of "Black is the Color of My True Love's Hair." I used to play that song for him on my guitar, back when we were both young.

Today, I turn forty-six.

I heave a sigh and stand. My true love will look thirty forever.

I pull off my T-shirt and cargo shorts, cuss a little at the nest of silver hair between my pecs, tug at my love-handles and cuss a little more, and then I climb into bed beside Derek. I roll him onto his side and lie facing him, fooling with the dark hair on his chest and belly, probing his navel, and caressing his limp cock. When I move closer and kiss him on his bearded chin, he smiles in his sleep.

I give my stiffening prick a few strokes before nudging him onto his back. On top of him, I suck hard on his nipples till they harden between my teeth. I slide lower and take his dick into my mouth.

For a few minutes, Derek just lies there, insensible, while I suck and lap his flaccid cock. Then it's thickening in my throat, and he shudders and his hands grip my head. The sun must have set.

"Nice way to wake up." I love the way he murmurs.

His hips buck against me; his cockhead pushes past my tonsils, and I nearly choke. "Keep that up, birthday boy," he sighs, holding my head harder. I obey; I love it when he tells me what to do. Grunting low in his throat, Derek fucks my face—slow, deep thrusts. I suck him and jack myself till my goatee's dripping with spit and I'm getting close to coming.

"You gonna rope me up and fuck me, Daddy?" I mumble around his shaft. I let his dick slip from my mouth only to lap the slit of it. "Give me a birthday spanking? Give me a birthday plowing?"

"Not this time," Derek says, gazing down at me, his brown eyes full of mischief. "I have a special surprise for you instead." He tugs my goatee and chuckles.

"You brought the silver cuffs? You gonna let me have a turn on top?" I say, cupping his butt-cheeks. "You want me up inside you? I'd sure like that. It's been a while since I got to fuck that tight little Highlander ass of yours."

"No. I have something else in mind." Derek pulls me up into his arms.

"Yeah?"

"Yes, indeed. Save your horned-up juice for later."

"Mmm, okay. You know I love surprises."

"And you know how much I like to treat you to the good life," Derek replies, raking a fang across my shoulder. We kiss and snuggle for a few minutes, tweaking tits and rubbing bellies and squeezing hard-ons before Derek rolls on top of me. We wrestle a little before he uses his greater strength to force my wrists above me.

"You got me now, Daddy," I say, wiggling beneath him. "I love your weight on top of me. I love how powerful you are, how you can master me so easy."

Derek laughs low. "I love it too. I love you, Matt. I could have taken you anywhere for your birthday. My new apartment in Rome. Key West. New York. London. Someplace elegant and expensive." He shoots a glance at the darkened window. "Why'd you choose Hawk's Nest?"

"Ah, just 'cause it'd been a while since I'd been here. My family used to come here for vacation. Guess I'm nostalgic for the old days, since I got no kin left to speak of. Just Cousin Dillon and that harpy sister of his, Darlene."

"Makes sense." Derek nuzzles my armpit. "You smell good." He sniffs like an eager hound dog. "I can't get enough of your scent. Did you go hiking today?"

"Sure did. And I brought you that." Unable to move my arms, I nod toward the bloodroot blossom on the table. "The woods are full of pretty wildflowers for my demon lover."

"A sweetheart of the first order." Derek smiles down at me and rubs his beard against my nose. "So you've had enough time here?"

"Yeah. Guess so. I walked all around. Went to that overlook where…"

I trail off. It's been hard getting used to the fact that the man I love is, every once in a while, a murderer. These days, he pretty much kills folks I'd classify as vermin—homophobes, gay-bashers, and rapists—but still, I grew up with "Thou shalt not kill" just like everybody else. That sort of thing sticks.

"The overlook where Cynthia and I drove Reverend Bates over the edge of the cliff?"

Derek snickers, clearly pleased with himself. I guess he's had nearly three hundred years to learn how to sidestep guilt. After all, he became a vampire just so's he could kill off the bastards that slaughtered his first love, Angus. He was born for retribution—it's in his blood. That's a kind of comfort. The big guy would take on the whole fucking world to protect me. The reason he got rid of Bates was 'cause the preacher's henchmen waylaid me, beat the hell out of me, and put me in the hospital. I might not approve of his methods sometimes, but his heart's sure in the right place.

"Yeah. *That* overlook." I bite his chin and start squirming. "So if you ain't gonna fuck me, you gonna let me up, monster man? I haven't eaten since breakfast. I'm famished. Where's that sumptuous birthday feast you promised me?"

"You're always famished. Something else we have in common." Derek releases me, then rubs the furry swell of my belly. "Time for dinner. Get dressed now." He slips off the bed, lifts the bloodroot blossom to his nose, then picks up the phone.

❧

We sit side by side on the twilit balcony and look out over the gorge. A few buzzards veer by. Derek sips Scotch from his flask, watching me as I tuck into bacon-wrapped filet mignon, baked potato, and broccoli with Hollandaise sauce. It's a highfalutin meal the restaurant staff created especially for me, thanks to Derek's persuasive mental powers. I smack my lips, add more sour cream and chives to my potato, and swig red wine from the bottle, feeling very cared for and very content.

By the time I'm done with dinner, the sky over the park is deep indigo, and the horizon is edged with the sun's last orange. I start into dessert, a fat slice of German chocolate cake, and polish it off fast. Spring peepers are cheeping somewhere, and the wind, chilly now, soughs through new leaves.

"I love watching you eat," Derek says. "Was it good?"

"It was fantastic. Thank you so much," I say, wiping my mouth and offering Derek the bottle of wine. "I'm stuffed. Been a long time since I've had steak that tasty. Medium-rare. Done just right."

Derek takes a long swig before handing the bottle back. "Good. That means I won't have to decapitate the cooks. I'd like to check out of here now."

"Now? We're driving all the way back home to Mount Storm tonight?"

"No. We're about to take a much shorter drive. The second act of your surprise." Derek moves to the railing and looks out over the gorge. "I don't want to stay here any longer. You can't feel them, can you?"

"Them?" I knock back the last of the wine. "'Them' who?"

"The ones who died here. When the tunnel was built. They tore at my sleep. They tattered my dreams. It felt as if they were gnawing my skin. Black bodies staggering across a snowy field, looking for their graves… They want something from me. Some sort of gesture. Some sort of offering. They want justice, I think. Vengeance. But it's too late. What can I do? The perpetrators are long dead."

I get what Derek means. It sure wasn't part of the West Virginia History course I took in eighth grade, but the story's gotten more attention since then.

There's even a marker near the overlook, explaining how, back in the 30's, a company hired a bunch of migrant workers, most of 'em black, to dig a big tunnel through this mountain to divert the New to make hydroelectric power. But the rock those poor guys bored through was pure silica, and hundreds of 'em came down with awful lung disease and eventually died.

"Were you in West Virginia back then?" I ask, joining him at the railing.

"Not much. I was in Europe during the thirties, trying to help a few Jewish vampires I'd taken a liking to sabotage the Nazi Party. As you might guess, we weren't very successful, thanks to some talented and malevolent German sorcerers who blocked us at every turn and even managed to slay a few of my compatriots. I barely escaped some foul elemental they sent after me."

"Damn. You never told me that."

"It was a bleak time, full of failure after failure. We did what we could, but it wasn't good enough. It felt as if history were against us. Hitler did as he pleased despite all our efforts. And then I fell in love with Gerard…"

He trails off. I know this story—the American soldier who died in '45 fighting the Nazis.

Derek takes my hand and kisses it. "Let's not talk about catastrophes any more. Let's leave this spectre-infested mountain and all talk of the doomed and the dead. It's time for another birthday gift. This treat is waiting for us just down the mountain, in Scrabble Creek."

☙

IT'S A BLEAK little holler, the road lined with shabby houses and trailers. I steer my pickup around one curve after another, following the creek. The hillsides, steep and wooded, tighten in around us as we ascend.

Derek points out a broke-down little church. "Snake handlers," he says.

"Shit," I say, rolling my eyes. "I'd be liable to piss myself. Only snakes I can tolerate are the ones you control, and them just barely."

Derek sniggers. "I know. You were damned glad to have me around last summer when you found that black snake wrapped around the wine rack, weren't you? There. Turn onto that dirt road there."

We bounce a good mile or so up the hill, moving deeper and deeper into woods, what's left of habitations dwindling down and disappearing behind us.

"My surprise is up here? Just looks like trees to me. Is it a fancy tree house?"

"It isn't a tree house, honey bear. There you go. Look."

Derek points and I see: on up the mountain, lights. I drive us another quarter of a mile, skirting a little brook, and we reach the end of the road, near the head of the holler. There's a trailer, with a pickup truck—a junky Ford, this one a lot worse for wear than mine—parked beside it. The porch light is on, and there's a light gleaming in the window at the far end.

"You bought me a vacation trailer?" I ask, patting his knee.

"Think of the trailer as the wrapping. The gift is inside," Derek says, opening the passenger door. "This is going to be sweet, I promise."

We climb out. The high cove's full of the brook's burble. We step up onto the porch. Derek doesn't bother to knock. He just opens the unlocked door.

"He's waiting for us," Derek says, ushering me inside. The interior's stuffy and musty, with all sorts of junk scattered around: fast-food wrappers, dumbbells, an empty gun rack, beer cans.

"Who's he?" I say, but at this point, I have some idea. One of Derek's more amazing powers is his ability to glamor guys.

"You'll see," Derek replies, locking the door behind us. He leads me down a narrow hallway, past a bathroom and a utility room and into a cramped bedroom.

The boy's sitting in low lamplight on the edge of the bed, gazing up at us. He's naked, and he's bound and gagged.

"This is Timmy Kincaid. He's been my thrall since February. Timmy, this is my husbear, Matt. Say hi."

Timmy isn't in a position to say anything. He's got duct tape plastered over his mouth. Instead, his blue eyes meet mine. He mumbles and gives a submissive little bow.

"Whoa! Howdy, man," I say. I'm already hard. Derek knows better'n anybody how much I like kink. "Damn glad to meet you. You're awful hot all tied up like that."

Timmy mumbles again, flexing his arms against the cords securing them to his sides. He's in his late twenties, I'd say, about my height, maybe a tiny bit taller. He's built like me: a little plump around the middle, with a nice set of muscles, a big chest and thick arms. He's hairy like me too, with a chestnut-brown pelt coating the entire front of his body. He's got a handsome face, with an unkempt brown goatee and bushy sideburns. Derek sure has a type, and it's my type too:

hairy, butch, bearded, and brawny. He knew I'd love this stocky little cub.

"So this is my present, huh?" I say, scratching my chin and studying the boy with horny relish. "He's like a younger version of myself."

Derek gives me a fanged smile. "Do you like him?"

"What the hell do you think?" I say, patting the bulge in my shorts. "Talk about right up my alley."

"Right up his alley is what I'm wanting to see," Derek says. "What are you waiting for? Tonight he's all yours. Aren't you, Timmy boy?"

Timmy nods. He stands, swaying on bound feet. He nods again and bows his head.

"Mmmmm." I stride over, grip the trussed-up boy's stiff prick and tousle his thick head of hair. He gazes at me, eyes vague and dreamy, then heaves a long sigh and leans against me. Several yards of rope circle his torso, arms, and elbows, and his hands are cuffed behind him. His cock isn't all that long, but it's sure thick, and hammer-hard with arousal. Both it and his balls have been tied up tight with a leather cord.

"Ain't you a tasty thang?" I say, tracking down a nipple in all that fur and roughly fingering it. "Nice big beefy pecs. Just the kind I like."

Timmy groans, pressing his chest against my hand. He clearly savors tit-work, which is great news, 'cause I love to work a bound man's nips about as much as I like my nips worked when I'm bound.

"You like this, huh?" I say, staring into his wide blue eyes and pinching his tit.

"Mmmm hmm," Timmy manages.

"His nipples are super-sensitive, just like yours," Derek says. "He'd like you to hurt them a little."

"You bet."

Dropping Timmy's dick, I take his nipples between my thumbs and forefingers and squeeze. He nods and sighs. I squeeze harder, and he winces and trembles. I increase the pressure till his eyes are full of pleading and pain. And gratitude, seems like. The boy rests his forehead against mine and mumbles low notes of what sounds like desperate thanks. He seems as hungry for all this as I am, though I don't know whether that's honest need or Derek's mind control.

"You have him broke in real nice," I say, leaving off the nip-work to pull Timmy into my arms. "Who can I thank for this pretty gift-wrapping?" I pluck at the tight ropes cinching the boy's elbows behind him.

"He tied himself up," Derek says. "Young Timmy takes orders well. Check his ass."

I do, patting the kid's fuzzy butt-cheeks and squeezing their solid roundness. When I slip a finger into his crack, I feel something hard.

"He asked me if a butt-plug would be all right. He said he wanted to be all lubed and open for you," Derek says. "I told him that was a grand idea."

"Yeah? Oh, damn. Yum." I nudge the plug, and Timmy moans.

"He told me he hasn't been fucked for a long time and he really needs to be plowed hard." Derek takes a seat in the corner of the room and folds his hands behind his head. "By both of us. 'I want to be bound and gagged and gang-banged, Lord,' that's the way he put it. Isn't that right, Timmy? You want both of us to use you?"

Timmy grunts and nods.

"You want both of us badly, don't you?" Derek says, his voice husky. He's rubbing his hard-on through his jeans. "You think Mr. Matt here is very sexy, don't you?"

Timmy grunts again, nodding more vigorously. He brushes his taped mouth against my face, as if trying to kiss me.

"Good boy," I say. I grip the plug and work it around a little. "Feel good?" In response, Timmy cocks his butt, bucks against me, and gives a long, low moan.

"So you ready to get fucked?" I say, kissing him on his tape-swathed cheek.

"Uhhh huh," he groans. "Uhhhh huhhhh." Bending from the waist, he thrusts his broad butt against my hand.

"So eager. Goddamn, nothing sweeter than a mountain man who wants a dick up his ass," I mutter. "Okay, boy, you got it. But first I wanna taste you all over."

I get naked fast, then push Timmy down onto the bed. I lie on top of him and kiss his face: his forehead, his thick eyebrows, his sideburns, his taped-up mouth, his goateed chin.

"Hell, you're a trussed-up treasure, ain't you?" I sigh, kneading his thick pecs before taking a hard nipple into my mouth. "Best birthday present yet."

"Glad you approve," Derek says. He has his shirt off now, and his dick out, stroking it.

I feast on Timmy's chunky pecs, lapping and chewing on the fur-shrouded little nubs while Timmy quivers and moans and Derek jacks himself. "Try these. He loves these," Derek says, tossing me a pair of taloned tit-clamps. When I ease them onto the boy's nips, he really starts to put up a fuss, thrashing around and heaving throaty little sobs. I twist and tug his clamped tits till his eyes are wet, then I move on down to his crotch to suck his bound-up cock and tug on his bound-up balls. The kid's really horned up and already close to coming, so I ease off his prick, roll him onto his belly, and slap his ass around till he's yelping against the mattress and his buttocks are nice and pink.

"Having a good time?" Derek asks, loosening his belt.

"Hell, yes. Our captive here's downright delicious." I sit on the bed's edge, haul Timmy's bulk onto my lap and give his butt another hard slap.

"He can take rougher. He loves a lengthy spanking. Use this." Derek tosses me his belt. "I want his pretty rump good and red when we take him."

I double it over and give Timmy a quizzical look. "You up for this?"

Timmy lifts his head, nods real emphatic-like, and props his butt in the air.

"Nice," I say. "You got it."

I beat Timmy slow and steady, the way Derek beats me when I bottom for him in scenes like this. For a while, the boy slumps in my lap, trembling and grunting and rubbing his hard-on against my thigh, but as the hurt builds he starts to tense up and struggle. His resistance just excites me more. I hold him down and whip his butt harder.

"Good job. Keep going," Derek says. "I want to see some tears."

"You want more?" I pause. "You want to cry?"

Timmy hesitates. He snuffles, breathing hard through his nose. He nods, clenches his cuffed hands, and wiggles his butt, inviting me to continue.

"Okay. Here we go."

It takes another ten minutes or so—the kid's a tough little shit—but finally our brawny captive breaks. Now he's writhing and shaking and choking up sobs.

"Beautiful, beautiful," Derek says. "That's enough."

"Man, you took a lot. More'n I could," I say. Arm aching, I drop the belt and kiss the kid's fiery butt-cheeks.

Derek stands. He slips off his boots, jeans, and briefs. He runs a hand over the boy's welted ass. "Ripe and red and ready to be raped. Let him loose, Matt."

I release Timmy. He slides off my lap, then falls to his knees by the bed. He gazes up at us, his masters for the evening, his good-looking face flushed with pain and surrender, his muscles bunching up as he flexes against his bonds. The tears that Derek's sadism craved rim his eyes and spill over his taped-up cheeks. Any guilt I might feel after treating him so rough is dismissed by the sight of his hard prick. I think he enjoyed himself even more'n I did.

Derek runs a hand over Timmy's face, wipes up the wet, and tastes the tears. "Good slave," he whispers, nudging Timmy's face with his cock. I do the same. Timmy nuzzles our erections as best he can, rubbing them with his gagged mouth and soft beard.

"You want these cocks up inside you now?" Derek says, pushing a lock of brown hair from Timmy's eyes.

"Mmmmmm!" The sound's muffled but affirmative. The glazed look of need in Timmy's eyes is one Derek's no doubt seen in mine: the raw lust of a man who wants to be mastered, who wants a big dick up his ass more'n anything in the world.

Derek lifts the boy to his feet. "Easy now," he says, bending him over and gently easing the butt-plug out. He fingers Timmy's hole a little before shoving him belly down onto the bed and handing me a tube of lube.

"All ready for you. Bareback him if you'd like. He's as free of disease as you are. I can smell it."

"Yeah? That all right with you, Timmy-boy?"

Timmy stares up at us. Head bobbing, he emits a long series of urgent-sounding syllables.

Derek chuckles. "Let me translate. That's well-gagged slave-talk for, 'Hell, yes. Shoot your loads in me. Make me your redneck come-dump.'"

"That's what he's saying? Jesus. That's fucking hot," I groan, greasing up my dick. I climb onto the bed, work some lube up Timmy's hole, and finger-fuck him for a few minutes while he squirms and whimpers, vulnerable little sounds sweet enough to break my heart. I roll Timmy onto his side, kiss his cheek, and push my prick up his ass.

☙❧

OUR THREE-WAY GOES on for most of the night, and every moment is sheer fucking bliss. I take Timmy hard and fast, thrusting in and out of top-notch tightness. Derek tugs his clamped nipples till they're raw, then replaces clamp-teeth with his fangs, drinking from the wincing boy's wounded tits till Timmy passes out. When he comes to, I bend him double and give him a slow, deep fuck on his back while Derek drinks from his neck. I come inside him with a bellow. After a few hours of napping and cuddling, Derek takes his turn on top, pounding the boy on his side while I suck his cock.

Less than a minute after Derek's finished inside him, Timmy's come in my mouth. I give Derek a big kiss, and we swap slave-semen back and forth before swallowing. Derek uncuffs Timmy and removes all the rope binding the boy's arms and torso—at this point, his shoulders are sure to be sore and stiff, and his wrists are chafed near to bleeding—then cuffs his hands before him for a more comfortable captivity. We sandwich our contented prisoner between us and drop off to sleep.

Near dawn, I wake to find Derek by the bed, pulling on his clothes. "Go back to sleep, honey," he says, kissing my forehead. "Spend the day with Timmy. Get to know him. He's had a hard life. I think he could do with a human friend. I've got to get farther away from these damn ghosts."

"They're here?"

"Yes. One in particular—a pale, emaciated man—is harassing me, making demands I can't understand. I'll be back after dusk."

I nod, roll over, and pull Timmy closer. He mumbles, tugs on my soft cock, and presses his face into my chest hair.

We sleep real late. When I wake again, afternoon sunlight's pouring through the trailer window. I lie there for a while, listening to the purling of the brook outside, admiring the bulky boy snoozing beside me, and then I lube myself up again. By the time Timmy wakes, I have my cock halfway up his ass. He moans happily and pushes back against me. Pretty soon I've dumped another load inside him, and he's shot all over the sheets.

I spoon him for a long time, fondling his sore nips, fuzzy belly, and limp cock. Finally, I help him sit up and proceed to pick the tape off his face, trying my best not to pull his beard too much. He flinches and cusses but keeps as still as he can. Beneath the tape, I find a couple yards of rope tied between his teeth, and beneath that, there's a balled-up Rebel flag bandana.

"Thanks!" Timmy gasps, once I've managed to remove all three layers of his gag. He licks his lips. "My jaw's sore. That was a mouthful. Please, man, could I have some water? I'm parched."

The side effects of blood loss. "Sure, bud. Let's get you into the kitchen."

I untie Timmy's feet and help him stand. He staggers some, and for a minute I think he's going to faint, but then he shakes the dizzy spell off. We look around for the handcuff key, but it's nowhere to be found. If I know Derek, he's deliberately kept the key in his pocket, and who knows what cave he might be sleeping in today? Far from here, I'll bet. Those ghosts really seem to have shaken him up.

I wrap an arm around Timmy. He leans against me as we make our way down the hall. Soon I have him sitting at the kitchen table gulping water, and I'm setting up his coffee machine.

"How's your butt?" I ask, pouring water into the carafe.

"Good. Real sore. You gave me a helluva beating."

"Sorry 'bout that. Derek insisted, and you know how persuasive he can be. I'll rub some lotion on you later, if you'd like. Your butt and nips and wrists look pretty torn up."

"I ain't complaining. I love a good beating. But lotion would be great. You're welcome to fuck me again too."

"I'd like that," I say, grinning. "You're a helluva ride."

Timmy blushes. "Don't mean to be greedy. I've just been real lonely lately. Derek won't be back till dark, right? So you're gonna hang out with me today?"

"Yep. Derek said you could do with a friend."

"That's the truth. Hey, sorry, I should be more hospitable and fix you breakfast, but…" He lifts his cuffed wrists and shrugs.

"Yeah, I get it. How about I cook us up something? What you got in the fridge?"

❧

Stuffed on bacon, eggs, and grits, we sprawl naked on the couch, Timmy's head in my lap. I fondle his fang-bruised pecs; he fools with the hair on my legs.

"Thanks. That was all tasty. It's sure good to have some company," Timmy sighs. "It feels great to snuggle with you. You're as sexy as Derek said."

"Thanks! Glad to be here. All this has been a super birthday surprise." I run my fingers through his shaggy goatee. "So Derek said you'd had a hard life. Wanna tell me about that?"

He nuzzles his head between my legs. "It's been a bunch of things. I grew up poor as dirt and lost my parents early. When folks roundabouts figured out I was gay, they got real hostile. Got my ass kicked a few times till I learned to fight. Finally found a boyfriend, but he up and left me, moved to DC. Got a good job in the mines, but when my bosses heard I was queer, they fired me. Been unemployed and lonely for months. Been drinking a lot, getting real depressed. By the time I met Derek, I was close to being evicted, had bills piled up to the ceiling, and…I hate to admit it, but I was thinking I'd be better off dead. Couple of times, driving up over Gauley Mountain or coming home from Charleston after striking out at the gay bar, I was tempted to steer over the side of the road and end it."

"Christ, that sounds awful," I say, squeezing his callused hand.

"It has been. I'd been feeling like I didn't have a body no more. Hadn't been touched or kissed or fucked for so long. Then Derek, he showed up at my door in a snowstorm, and he, well, he beat me up, and then he tied me up…"

I can't help but snicker. "He does tend to do that."

"Yeah, he left me on the floor, tied up all day and gagged. I thought he was gonna come back and kill me. I shouted myself hoarse. I even pissed myself! Finally he showed up, and he bit me, and he made love to me. Damn, he was so savage and sweet. I gotta admit…I'm a little in love with him. He woke my body up. I'd do anything for him. I want him to take me to bed and do whatever he wants. Does that bother you? Am I making any sense?"

"You're making perfect sense. You're what he calls a thrall. You know what he is, right?"

"Yeah, I know." Timmy pats a bite mark on his right pec. "I know why I feel so weak today. He drinks from me." He drops his head and stares at the floor. "I want him to drink from me."

"Of course."

"He could drink me dead, and I'd be fine with that."

"He's not gonna drink you dead, I promise. So how much of what you feel for him is real, and how much is 'cause of his power?"

"Don't know. I had nothing to live for till I met him, and now I look forward to his visits like crazy, in real life and in my dreams. Is that all right with you?"

"Sure, that's fine. Derek likes to have his extra tidbits. I don't mind, 'cause I know he loves me."

Why do I say this? I suppose I'm staking a claim. Timmy's face crumbles. I pat him on the pec. "He's good about sharing."

"Glad you are too. He's been real good to me. He told me if he owned me, he'd take care of me, and he has. Right after I told him that Alpha Coal fired me, their office burnt down. I've been too afraid to ask him if he did it. I'd be thanking him, though. He's left me cash that's kept me from being homeless."

"He can be generous. How about s'more coffee? Then I'll lotion up those sore spots of yours."

✧

OF COURSE ONE thing leads to another, and we spend the rest of the day in bed. Turns out we're both pretty versatile when dominant Derek isn't around, so Timmy and I take hearty turns butt-fucking one another. It's in the snuggling after-play that he gets to talking about his Fayette County family roots, and that's when I find out something Derek needs to know.

I've got Timmy on his elbows and knees, screwing him from behind, when Derek pulls one of his dramatic entrances, misting into the room and materializing. After I've come in Timmy's ass, Derek's come in Timmy's mouth, and Timmy's come in Derek's mouth, it's time to pop the news.

"So did you get away from the ghosts?" I ask. Timmy's sandwiched between us again, sighing with satisfaction.

"I did. I slept in a grotto above Montgomery." Derek grimaces. "But I can still feel them. They're here, whispering unintelligible demands."

"I think I know what they want. I think they want Timmy to move in with us. To be our house-cub till he gets back on his feet."

"Really?" Derek grins. "Did you two hit it off that well?"

"We did, Sir. But, Matt, that's a big step. Are you sure y'all—"

"I'm sure. The ghosts of those guys don't want retribution. They want kindness. At least one of 'em does."

Derek frowns. "How do you know that?"

"Timmy, tell Derek what you told me. About your ancestor."

Timmy bites his lip. "Okay. So, I ain't the first member of my family chewed up and spit out by big industry. My great-granddaddy was one of the workers who dug the Hawk's Nest Tunnel. Died at age twenty-eight, shrunk down to a skeleton. Pretty much suffocated to death, his lungs eaten up with silicosis and tuberculosis. He ended up in a cemetery near Gauley Bridge. Most of his black buddies were buried in mass graves."

Derek's eyes widen. "What was his name?"

"Callum Kincaid."

"Callum. Yes. That's his name. He's here now."

"Oh, shit," Timmy whispers. "Great-Granddaddy's here?"

Derek stands. "Keep quiet, boys. Let me focus."

A long moment passes. There's no sound but the burbling creek, and even that for a few seconds seems to stop.

Derek nods. Bending, he slips the cuff key from his discarded jeans. He pulls Timmy to his feet, unlocks the cuffs, and stares into his eyes.

Timmy swallows hard, shudders, staggers, and sits heavily on the bed. He bows his head and kneads his chafed wrists. He looks up at Derek and rubs his brow hard. "What happened?" he asks, clearly stunned.

"Now you're free to do as you please," Derek says, taking a few steps backward.

"Yeah? Wow. Yeah." Timmy stands. "Is Great-Granddaddy still here?"

Derek shakes his head. "No. He's gone. They're all gone. Matt was right."

I clamber out of bed and thump Timmy's shoulder. "You ain't Derek's slave now. You got your will back. Wanna join our family? Wanna come home with us?"

"You're sure y'all want that?"

"We do," Derek says. "If you do."

Timmy digs his knuckles into his temples. He looks us both up and down. "Yeah. Yeah, I do," he says, sounding surprised. "I'd like that a lot."

"Tomorrow," Derek says, "I'll buy this land. You'll have it to come back to if you change your mind."

"That would be cool. Thank you, Sir."

"Sir? You don't need—"

"I want to," Timmy says. "Feels right. So when we leaving? Ain't like I got much to pack."

"If we leave soon," I say, slipping an arm around Timmy's waist, "we'll be home before dawn. I can make us a big Welcome-to-Mount-Storm buckwheat-cake breakfast while Derek snoozes."

"Sounds great. I'm starved." Timmy beckons to Derek. "Speaking of which, come on over here, Sir. You must be hungry."

Derek raises an eyebrow. "Are you sure?"

"I'm sure. I know what I'm doing now. I trust you. You ain't gonna hurt me."

"Drink from me too," I say. "Spread that Daddy-love around."

Timmy and I step into his embrace. We lean against Derek as he nuzzles our necks and caresses our buttocks. All three of us are hard again.

"Nothing's better'n this, brother," I whisper, gripping Timmy's cock. "Cherished and protected by power. It's worth any price."

Timmy nods drowsily, smiles, and closes his eyes. With a gravelly growl, Derek pulls us close, eager to take the love and youth his body craves.

THREE

VANILLA
'NATHAN BURGOINE

My grandmother had always told anyone who'd listen—which had been anyone who wanted something sweet from her store—that I had a "touch of the fey." People smiled as she extolled the virtues of my deft hands while pouring hazelnut clusters into her signature cream and yellow boxes. They nodded while she sliced her triple chocolate fudge and bragged about my latest—and financially fruitless—art showing. She would point to the small painting I'd done for her—an abstract inspired by the rich browns and honey colours of her chocolates—and ask them if it didn't make their mouth water.

It did, her customers would agree, maybe even slightly alarmed that it was true. Then they'd take their purchase and go home.

I'd arrived from Vancouver on the first flight I could get. Her neighbor had decided to call me despite my grandmother's wishes that nobody "bother" me with her troubles. I'd been by her side, holding her hand, while she maintained almost to the last moment that she wasn't worth the fuss, and that I should go home.

Standing in Sweet Temptations, I reached out and touched the counter. I drew a line in the light coating of dust that had formed. It was barely visible, really. I waited.

"Well?" I said. I wasn't sure who I was asking. My grandmother, perhaps, or maybe...

The mark in the dust shifted. Lines formed, like frost on a cold window, and spread across the countertop. If it hadn't been dust, it would have been a stunning pattern—a kind of spider web in motion. Instead, it was merely pretty.

I nodded. "Okay," I said. "Let's give this a try."

I went to find my grandmother's mop and bucket.

✿

LIKE EVERY OTHER attempt at finding some permanent direction for my life I had tried, I decided to give the chocolate shop my complete attention. It didn't take long to sub-let my apartment in Vancouver, and I moved into the small home above the storefront that my grandmother had lived in. I was officially living in the Village, the few blocks of Bank Street that formed the gay strip of Ottawa.

I was outside the store, cleaning the windows, when the first local stopped me. She was an older woman with obvious taste, wearing an ivory blouse and classy touches of understated gold jewellery, and walked with a lovely hand-carved wooden cane that had probably cost a tidy sum. A small puff of air escaped her mouth as she lowered herself onto the bench outside the store. She nodded at me.

"Is the store reopening soon?" There was a slight tremble to her voice.

I nodded. "My grandmother left it to me. I have her recipes, and when I was younger, I used to help out."

"I'm sorry for your loss," she said. Then she smiled at me. "But wait, that means you're Avery!"

I nodded again. "That's me."

"You look nothing like your photograph," she said, with a wink.

I smiled. I'd found a picture of myself in a frame near the cash register. It had been taken when I was about thirteen years old, on Hallowe'en of all nights, dressed as a pumpkin. I'd been holding up a candy and screwing up my face, thoroughly disgusted by what had passed for a treat at other homes.

Having a grandmother who was a fine chocolatier did sort of take the fun out of trick or treating.

The woman laughed. "She was a lovely woman."

"Thank you," I said.

She took a breath, and began to struggle her way to standing again. I reached out, and she took my hand and help gratefully.

"Getting older," she said. "It's not for sissies."

"Neither is being a sissy." I winked, and she laughed again. As she walked away, she didn't seem to notice that she was carrying her cane instead of using it.

⚜

THE DAY I re-opened, it was a zoo. I'd known that my grandmother was a lovely woman, but I'd had no idea the sheer volume of people she'd "adopted" as her own. She had always been like that. I felt a surge of familial pride—and a little guilt—that so many people dropped by to tell me how much they'd loved her. Nearly everyone also bought a few things, or asked me if I was going to make a particular recipe from my grandmother's repertoire that I hadn't thought to try for the re-opening. I'd been worried I'd have my usual luck, and had scaled the range of the chocolates back as much as I dared. Instead, I was getting orders and promises from people to come back later for my grandmother's famous pecan points, or the coconut snowballs—apparently a Glebe tradition among the older clientele at their bridge gatherings.

When the delivery came, I'd been pouring the last few dark chocolate cherries into one of the cream and yellow boxes for a handsome man in his mid-thirties.

"My wife swears this is the only thing that can get her through morning sickness," he said. "She was almost in a panic when we found out we were pregnant again and this shop was closed."

I thanked him, and turned to look at the next customer, which was when I realized the next customer wasn't a customer at all. The notable head-to-toe brown of his uniform was obvious enough, but I hadn't seen someone pull off the look quite so well before. He was stocky, probably had a decade or two on me, and had his brown hair cut almost military short. He lifted two large packages, one in each hand, by the thick string that was tied around them. His biceps thickened with the effort.

I tried not to stare.

"You want these in the back?" he asked. It was obvious he'd been here before. I blinked. "Uh," I said.

He smiled, small lines forming around his eyes. "These are those yellow boxes. Emily had me pop them onto the shelves for her. They're pretty heavy, though I guess you can probably handle it yourself."

It was weird to hear someone call my grandmother by her name. My tongue re-engaged. I gestured to the door that led into the back. "Go right ahead, if you wouldn't mind. I'm struggling to keep up." As if cued, another couple came to the counter. I glanced at the delivery guy's wide back as he shouldered the door open, and then reluctantly turned back to the young couple at the counter, slicing some fudge for them, and wrapping it in wax paper. When they left, a teenager stepped up for an order of coconut snowballs—I added her to the list—and she sighed theatrically when I apologized for not having any ready.

After she had gone, I realized the delivery man was still standing there, holding the electronic pad for me to sign.

"Right," I said, and took the little stylus from him.

"You bought the place?" he asked.

"I inherited it," I said, and handed the pad back to him.

"You're Avery?" He sounded surprised.

I nodded. "I'm Avery."

His lips quirked. It was a good look on him—he had a strong chin. I wondered if he'd shaved this morning or if he was just one of those guys who got a half-day head start on their five o'clock shadow no matter how often they used a razor.

"You don't look like your picture," he said.

I groaned. "That pumpkin costume..."

He laughed. "I'm Vic." He offered his hand. "Your grandmother talked a lot about you."

We shook. Then another customer came, and he was gone before I could say anything else. When I finally closed the shop for the night, realizing I was about to spend many hours that night baking if I was to have any hope of catching up on the most requested inventory, I decided that it couldn't hurt to order more boxes.

Just in case.

"Looks like business is good."

I handed the customer her pecan points and nodded to the man who'd spoken. He was dark haired, and very handsome—almost a model's looks—with a perfect smile and eyes the colour of Belgian chocolate. He was dressed in a crisp white collared shirt and navy pants.

"It's been a good first week," I admitted. I was understating, but nervous. I'd had flash-in-a-pan success before. "May I help you?"

"I'm Pete Marlin. I own Bittersweets, down in the Byward Market," the man said, holding out his hand. I quickly wiped my hand on a towel, and then shook. "The previous owner used to sell some of her products at my coffee shop, and she carried small packs of my coffee. I heard that the place had re-opened. I didn't know if you were going to run the place the way she did, but it was a mutually beneficial arrangement."

"My grandmother wasn't the world's greatest bookkeeper. I'm sorry—I didn't know the two of you had an arrangement."

He blinked. "You're Avery?"

I sighed. "Why does everyone say it like that?"

Pete chuckled. "You just don't look like the picture."

"I was a kid! In a pumpkin costume! I swear to God I sent her more recent photos."

Pete smiled, looking at me for a long moment. Another customer entered the store and I excused myself to send her on her way with some white chocolate raspberry shards, but then another couple entered, and after that there were more.

Pete waved to me, near the door. "I'll come by another time," he called out. "I keep good records. I can go over it with you."

I nodded to him. "That'd be great."

He stepped out the door, and a few minutes later when I looked up again, I saw he was still outside, now talking with Vic. They seemed to be having an animated discussion, and I wondered how they knew each other. I couldn't quite break away long enough to get near the door, and by the time I'd finished with the small customer rush, Vic was walking in with a bag of cocoa powder under his arm and a grin on his face.

"Got something big and sweet for ya," he said.

I laughed, and signed, and watched him go. I'd taken the opportunity to check something this time.

No wedding band.

※

I'D BEEN UP late baking, and had gotten up early to accomplish more. The coconut snowballs hadn't turned out right the night before—I'd over-thought the process—but the second batch I'd made this morning had the right consistency, and held together. I'd been thinking about how I'd watched my grandmother make them as a child, and had helped roll the balls before they grew too cool to shape. She'd said my hands always knew what they were doing, even if I didn't.

"So the statue in the window," Vic's voice broke my tired reverie. "That's you, right?"

I blinked. I hadn't even heard him come in. Man I was beat. "Yeah. I took a sculpting class during my first career."

"First career?" Vic put down the package. It was cane sugar.

"Artist," I said. "Painted, sculpted, carved…I tried it all. It didn't work out." This was putting it mildly. At my first art showing, I'd sold a moderate number of pieces, and attracted attention from the art scene. I'd been excited—thinking I'd found my calling. I'd put on a professional show and the critics had been unanimous. The work was powerful. Impressive, even. But they all thought it was somehow overwhelming. In fact, bringing one of my pieces into your home was pretty much guaranteed to wreck your room, they said, and be the only thing in it that anyone ever noticed. In short: my art belonged in museums, perhaps, but they sure didn't want them for their houses. People had stared at my sculptures, discussed them in quiet whispers, and I'd stood there, realizing that once again, my hands had produced something a bit too…much.

Vic jerked his thumb towards the statue. "No one liked that?"

"That was a final project in one of my sculpting classes. I got a B minus," I said. I'd carved the sculpture out of stone, and then given it a faux marble finish that looked as good as real. It was a lean chest and torso—mine, actually—reclining. We'd been asked to mirror classic statuary. My prof had told me it was borderline offensive in its suggestiveness. I hadn't been aiming for anything of the sort, but even he couldn't deny I'd followed the right style. Hence the B minus. I'd had the sculpture sent from my apartment, not wanting it to get ruined by the sub-letter.

Last night I'd had the idea to put it in the window, and drizzle some chocolate across the sculpture's chest. Hey, it made for an interesting window display, and if it caught some attention, that could only be a good thing. Having to re-stock almost the entire ingredient list of all my grandmother's recipes hadn't been cheap, and the initial buzz of the re-opening had died down to a more steady level now, though I was still busy.

"No accounting for taste," Vic said. "Bet half your customers want to lick the chocolate right off."

I was inspired. "Maybe I could make little body chocolate kits."

"People would buy that," Vic said.

I regarded him. I could never quite tell if he was flirting with me. He seemed to have some off-hand comment to toss at me every time he came, and the way he looked at me... Still. He was a masculine guy, and rough around the edges. I wasn't sure about him at all.

"Would you?" I asked, and then felt my face heat up.

Vic leaned forward, and to my surprise, he reached out and tugged the front of my shirt collar down.

"It's fine for you," he said, then smiled. "But anyone licking chocolate off me would get a mouth full of hair." He let go of my shirt, and pulled at his own collar, revealing dark hair, and the start of his thick chest muscles, just below the throat.

I tried not to stare. I also hoped that my work pants—which were a bit snug—weren't revealing my obvious response to the feel of his finger at my neck.

"Well," I said finally. "You wouldn't have to be the plate."

Whatever response Vic might have made was interrupted when the door opened to admit Pete with a folder tucked under his arm.

"Avery," Pete said. "Finally, a moment when you're not doing anything important."

That was an odd way to put it. I glanced at Vic and saw him shake his head a little. He turned. "See you tomorrow," he said to me, and headed for the door.

I watched him go, and noticed that he brushed Pete as he went, giving him a less than gentle nudge. Pete didn't react. He approached the counter.

"Let's talk coffee beans and dark chocolate," he said, and winked at me.

We spoke for almost an hour, going over the arrangement my grandmother had had with him. He was free with his touches, often tapping my forearm or touching my shoulder. We changed a few minor details Pete had admitted he'd put in so he'd not overwhelm my grandmother.

"I think you could keep up with me, though," he said, with one of his killer smiles. Basically, I was going to carry a small selection of his coffees, and he'd carry some of my treats. We'd generate some traffic flow into each other's stores, and given the sales history, Pete considered it a win-win. I liked the idea, and was happy to give it a go.

As he rose, he held out his hand, and we shook.

"You let me know if there's anything you need, okay, Avery?" He smiled again, and I couldn't help but notice that this time he wasn't wearing a dress shirt, but had chosen a snug black t-shirt. It adeptly showed off how fit he was, and made his eyes seem all the darker.

"Okay," I said, and then Pete left, giving me one more wink at the door.

I went to the small marble countertop behind the displays and sprinkled icing sugar across the surface. I'd make some chocolate dominoes, I decided, still wondering about Pete's wink.

"Is it just me," I said to the empty store, "or has the metrosexual revolution really muddied up the waters?" I looked down and saw that the icing sugar had arranged itself in delicate lines and angles all across the marble. It looked like hieroglyphics.

"Thanks," I said. "That clears things right up."

❦

HONEYCOMB, TO SWEETEN *the tongue*, I thought, then paused.

What was I thinking? I put down the glass jar and took a shaky breath. Then I picked up the small bottle of ground chilli powder.

To enflame passion.

I bit my lip. It was late, and I'd been starting to feel light-headed for the last hour or so, but now…I was acting almost on autopilot.

"No you weren't," I said. "Be honest." I looked at the dried chilli powder, and felt a kind of warmth in my fingertips.

I'd never actually tried to use my touch before. It wasn't something I'd ever really considered attempting. But Vic and Pete were driving me mental. Every delivery seemed to be another opportunity for Vic to say some loaded thing, but he didn't go far enough to actually ask me out. And Pete was somehow worse—I was never sure if he was asking me if I wanted to add more products to his coffee shop, or if he was waiting for me to offer to bring something a whole lot sweeter to the table. One thing was for sure, I wasn't about to make the first move with my delivery guy. Or a business partner. That seemed like a really bad idea.

Honeycomb would make them speak, I knew with some vague instinct, but it would also inspire flattery. Exaggeration.

"No," I said. "That's not quite right." I picked up the jar of honeycomb, and put it back on the shelf. I closed my eyes, and remembered my grandmother's voice. *Your hands know what they're doing, even if you don't.*

A mix of passion and honesty, then. Not honeycomb. Not with chilli powder. I reached out my hand, tracing across the bottles and containers and jars with one finger. I felt a kind of thrill in my stomach. Neither of the two men might be interested in me. Hell, for all I knew, they were both just being polite—or looking for a good business deal, in Pete's case. "How do you get someone to tell you the truth?" I said.

My finger stopped. Vanilla. I picked up the jar and started working before I could change my mind.

༄

"I'm thinking of calling them Hot Chocolates," I said. My hands were fists in my pockets, and the small tray of chocolates was on the counter between Vic and myself. My heart was hammering in my chest.

"They're cute," Vic said, looking at them. I'd shaved and sculpted chocolate shells in the shape of a tall cup, filled them with the mousse, and sprinkled a few tiny pieces of white chocolate flakes over the top. They looked for all the world like tiny mugs of hot chocolate, with marshmallows.

"Try one," I said. I tried to sound casual.

"Your grandmother never gave free samples," Vic said, picking up one of the chocolates. It looked small in his hand, and oddly delicate. I flinched when Vic popped it into his mouth and chewed it quickly.

Vic grunted. "It's sort of spicy…" He swallowed and licked his teeth. "Really good though. Not what I expected." He blinked.

The door opened.

I turned, surprised. Pete arrived with packets of coffee in a box. He wasn't due for another hour.

"Quiet morning," Pete said, reading my expression. "I figured I'd drop them off now." He put the box on the counter.

"It's threatening rain out," I said. I looked at Vic nervously. The big man was looking at Pete. I might have imagined it, but it might *almost* have been described as glaring.

"It's really good," Vic said again, and then turned to Pete. "Try one of these."

"Uh—" I started, but Pete popped the Hot Chocolate into his mouth and chewed before I could think of an appropriate reason to deny him.

This wasn't the plan.

"It's spicy," Pete said, and coughed, but he was smiling. He chewed. "Good though. It's…" He coughed again. "Spicy."

Vic thumped him on the back. "You're a wuss. This is why I always win." Then he blinked, as if surprised.

"You win because you cheat, you bastard," Pete shot back, licking his finger. "You've probably been telling Avery I have lice." Then he shook his head, and as one, they both looked at me.

"What," I said slowly, "are you two talking about?"

Vic's neck was flushed. "We…were sort of competing…for you."

I stepped out from behind the counter. "Come again?"

Pete smiled. "Your grandmother told us you were gay. She tried to set us both up for a date with you whenever you visited, but the picture—"

I groaned. "The fucking pumpkin photo."

Vic nodded. "But the first morning I saw you…Damn." He stepped toward me. I froze. "You're hot. And that statue…" Vic shook his head. "You said it was you, right?"

I nodded.

"Made me want to bend you over the counter and do you right there and then."

"Oh," I said weakly. Vanilla. For honesty. Well. That seemed to be working.

"When he saw me coming out of the store he said he saw you first and I should back off," Pete said. "But…well, he's right. You're hot. So we made a deal."

"A deal," I repeated weakly.

"Whoever got you first keeps you. The other backs off," Pete said. "But you had to make the first move."

I stared at the two men. "I think I'm offended."

Vic smirked, "No you're not. You've got a hard on. Again."

I felt my face heat up. I absolutely needed looser fitting work pants.

"Typical," Pete said. He took a step away. "Lucky bastard."

"It's not luck," Vic grinned.

"No, wait," I said. Pete stopped, and then gave Vic a wide smile.

"You're kidding," Vic said. "You like him?"

I raised his hands. "No. Well, yes. But no…just wait. I'm not…I mean, I don't…" I stepped away from the two men, to the front door of the shop. I put my back to it, eyeing them as if they were wild animals. I glanced at the little plate of Hot Chocolates. What had I been thinking?

"The chocolates…" I started, and then stopped. What exactly was I going to say? *My grandmother always said I had magic hands. Those chocolates? I made them by hand and used vanilla to figure out if either of you were gay. Which, it turns out, you both are. The chilli powder, by the way, might have been going a step too far. That's why you're both so horny.*

Yeah. Not going to happen.

Pete picked one of the hot chocolates up. So did Vic. They walked over to me, and I felt my entire body shiver. They were both really hot in their own way, and they were looking at me like I was edible.

Oh man.

Pete offered the chocolate to me, held between his thumb and forefinger, an inch from my lips. I opened up and leaned forward, taking the chocolate and Pete's fingertip into my mouth.

They were right. It was spicy, but very good. A great mix. I licked at Pete's fingertip, then Pete pulled his hand back. I chewed. Swallowed.

"That," I said, "was a really bad idea."

Pete raised an eyebrow.

I felt the warmth in my throat, and a flush crept up my neck. It also settled lower, where I was already feeling more than enough warmth.

Vic held out his Hot Chocolate, but before I could open my mouth, the big man tugged at the neckline of my shirt and crushed the chocolate into the hollow of my throat.

"Oops," Vic said, a wicked smile on his face. Then he bent low and licked off the mess. His tongue was hot against my skin, and the chocolate melted under Vic's mouth.

I gasped.

Vic straightened. "Well?" he said, in his deep rough voice.

I reached awkwardly behind me and flipped the sign to closed. I fumbled at the lock until it snapped.

"I can't decide," I said, and tasted vanilla truth on my tongue. "I want you both."

The two men looked at me. Slowly, they smiled.

I led them out of the store front and into the kitchen.

∽

VIC'S HANDS WERE tugging at my shirt from behind while Pete held my face and gave me a kiss that curled my toes. We broke apart just long enough for Vic to pull my shirt over my head, and then we kissed again, his tongue still hot with the taste of chocolate and chilli powder. Vic pressed into me from behind, his arousal obvious against my back, and his rough hands slid around my stomach. His leaned into me, and his stubbled chin rubbed against my neck as he ran his hands up and down my bare chest, stopping to flick at each nipple.

I let out a little groan, and he turned me around. Vic's kiss was rougher than Pete's, and his tongue more intrusive. Behind me, I felt Pete step back, and his shirt tossed to the side glimpsed from the corner of my eye. When Vic came up for air, I turned. Pete's lean body was cut and smooth. I reached out and ran one hand across his stomach, feeling the muscles there.

Vic began to unbutton his brown uniform shirt, shedding it quickly. His stocky body was hairy, like I remembered glimpsing, with a thick chest and strong arms. I rubbed my other hand across Vic's body.

It was like a signal. They both moved at me, and we half collided against the large slab table. Kissing them in turn, I felt their hands at my back, at my chest, rubbing and touching me, and all the while I was breathless from losing myself to their tongues.

"Wait," I said, nearly gasping the word. The two men pulled back just slightly, the three of us mashed against the countertop. Their eyes were locked on me, Vic's hazel, and Pete's rich dark brown. "I want to watch you two," I said. Vanilla washed through my mouth, followed a moment later by the hot burn of chilli powder.

The two men looked at each me a moment longer, then took a half step back, turning to face each other and then leaning in for a slow kiss. Vic's hand slid up Pete's lean chest, until his finger and thumb found the man's nipple, and he gave it a slight pinch. Pete arched his back, and Vic started to lick down Pete's chin, and then his neck.

Pete moaned.

I undid my belt, and tugged my zipper down, sliding my pants down while I watched the two men rub against each other. Pete took a turn licking Vic's neck, and then moved his face down onto the large man's chest, pressing himself against the big man's hairy body.

"Yeah," Vic said.

I stepped out of my pants, and the two men heard the belt buckle click against the cool tile floor. They looked at me, standing there in my boxers, hard on obvious, and grinned at me. Vic moved first, his thick arms hooking around my waist and lifting me bodily onto the slab table. Then Pete was there, too, his hand snaking around the back of my head and pulling me against his chest. I licked at the nipple Vic had teased, and Pete let out a breathy moan.

Vic lifted me, tugging at my boxers and pulling them down and off with his rough hands, and then unzipping his uniform pants. Pete let me go, and I watched the two of them strip the rest of the way—Pete's smooth stomach ended with a small patch of hair above his long, curved cock, while Vic's stocky frame had a pair of hairy balls and thick uncut dick to match. They kicked their pants awkwardly off over their shoes, and stood watching me for a moment.

"Hi," I said, and laughed. They grinned, and step forward.

Vic knelt in front of the table, and lifted my legs. His hot tongue and rough chin pressed against my ass. Pete bent over, and took my hard dick into his mouth, sucking my head and shaft in one smooth motion. My head rocked back and I gasped. Their mouths worked me, Vic's tongue teasing and probing at me, while Pete's massaged my length and swirled around my cockhead. I found myself gasping and writhing under their combined attention, heard myself let out a warning cry just in time. Pete took my cock in his hand for the final two strokes, and Vic pushed his tongue deep into me.

I shot across my stomach, the spray of white the mirrored opposite to the dark chocolate drizzled across the chest of the statue in the front window. I lay back for a moment, breathing, then slowly shifted to slide myself off the slab table.

Vic and Pete frowned at me at first, but when I sank to my knees and urged Vic to stand again, he rose. I wrapped a hand around each of their hard cocks, and stroked them. They pressed in against me, and I started to suck Pete while I jerked Vic, alternating back and forth between the two. Pete's cock was long, and harder to swallow, but Vic's thick meat was no easy task either. I moved back and forth between the two men, and they wrapped one arm around each other's shoulders while they stood above me. I bobbed my head faster and faster, and soon both men were making low noises.

Pete shot first, fast spurts that sprayed across my chin and chest, but Vic followed soon after, with a hot wet surge that burst across my lips and dripped down into my lap. The two men leaned heavily against the slab table, and I pressed my back against one of its legs. We all breathed heavily, panting to catch our breath.

"So," Pete said. "You guys wanna maybe get a cup of coffee sometime?"

I laughed.

"Fuck," Vic swore. "Hell yes."

The two men stepped back. I rose shakily, and handed them both a clean towel to rub themselves with, and then they gathered their shed clothes. I wiped myself down as best I could, and found my boxers. They were dressed before I was, and waited for me to tug on my shirt and pants.

"I'll let you guys out," I said. "I need to have a quick shower before I open the shop again." Both men grinned at me, more than a little smug.

I locked the door after them, and leaned against the glass.

"Thank God I didn't use the honeycomb," I said, then went to have a shower.

INVASION
ROB ROSEN

THE ALIENS SETTLED in Africa and Europe—what with their love of giraffes and Alpine skiing, and all—and forced the previous inhabitants to move out. In return, they offered us a cure for cancer and put a stop to global warming. It seemed like a fair trade, all things considered, until the newly-evicted neighbors, ergo a third of the planet, started arriving in droves and you realized just how necessary a daily shower and a stick of deodorant really were.

Though, to be fair, none of us really had that much say in the matter.

See, the aliens' planet had been enveloped by a nearby super nova and ours was the closest thing to a home that they could find—never mind that our world was already occupied, not to mention precariously so, and that we would've greatly preferred a long distance relationship with them. Still, considering their superior intellect, not to mention weaponry, we rolled out the red carpet, unloaded a few thousand welcome baskets and promptly resettled two entire continents. Easy peasie.

On the bright side, I always did oh-so-love Italian men. Too bad that by that point in time the rest of the world oh-so-hated any and all Americans. In other words, though we now had to live with one another, we didn't have to like it. Or even pretend to.

As for the aliens, once they demonstrated their military might and informed us of their plans, we only ever had verbal contact with them. Naturally, rumors immediately began to spread as to what they looked like. I, personally, was hoping for the little green men scenario to pan out. It was high time to add to our rather boring pallet of white, black, brown, red and yellow.

What I wasn't counting on, however, was a first-hand encounter.

Or a first-cock encounter, as was the case.

I was standing naked in my bedroom, casually stroking a fat boner while I spied on my new German neighbor through a gap in my blinds. Hans didn't believe in rolling up his shades or wearing clothes when he was at home. With a small set of binoculars, I could easily watch him walk around his house, his hefty schlong swaying back and forth as he absentmindedly tugged on his foreskin.

And that's when I spotted it.

Out of a corner of my eye—well, a corner of the lens, actually—I noticed a pinprick of bright light. I set the binoculars down and looked to my left, out to my backyard. My heart began a fast *kerthump* as I watched in stunned amazement a small silver craft float down and silently land. One minute it was a blip in the blue sky, the next a parking violation.

It seemed that E.T., apparently, didn't feel the need to phone ahead. Still, I slipped on my robe, waited a few seconds for my prick to go semi, and nervously walked outside. Sure I was scared as hell, but equally just as curious. So much speculation had been swirling about as to their appearance, and I was about to find out the truth, even if it killed me.

"Please don't kill me," I mumbled to myself as the door to the ship slid up. Out of the inner light he appeared, dressed all in white and, much to my surprise, very un-alien looking. In fact, he looked quite a bit like Matt Lauer from the *Today Show*, except with noticeably more hair on his head.

"Greetings, Earthling," he said, a broad smile plastered across his handsome face as he emerged from his ship and walked over, his hand held out in greeting.

"Oh, um, hi," I replied, my own hand trembling as I shook his. "Welcome to, um, New Jersey."

He looked around my yard, his head in a tilt. "What was the old Jersey like?"

I laughed, despite the circumstances, which, if not dire, were at least pretty odd at best. "A lot less polluted and not as much traffic, I suppose," I answered, releasing his hand and standing back to get a good look at him. And, my, he did indeed look good. "So, what brings you to my humble home? If you were looking for Manhattan, you missed it by a couple of exits."

Again he smiled with those dazzling pearly whites. "I was scanning this area when my sensors picked up a certain heat level I was seeking to study."

I glanced at my outdoor Jacuzzi and said, "Well, it is heated, but I bet your technology goes way beyond blowing bubbles."

He laughed, emitting a deep rumble that ran up and down my spine and sent my balls swaying. "No, Earthling. The heat my ship sensed came from there." He pointed to the center of my robe, which he unknotted and parted. A blush spread up my neck and across my cheeks as he waved his slender finger at my flaccid penis. "Before I arrived, I believe this area was in a state of arousal. I seek to study this."

I closed my robe up tight. "You want to study my dick?"

He nodded his head. "In general, yes. Human sexual behavior, in particular. You see, our world is exceedingly far away from yours, so that while we know about your planet, we know little about the creatures that roam it."

"And yet you look remarkably like us," I couldn't help noticing.

"Yes, this is true. The building blocks of life are similar from planet to planet. Our two worlds evolved much in the same way, hence our physical similarities. Our evolution, however, started many millennia before your own."

"Which is why you were so easily able to take over our world and all we could do was allow it."

His smile wavered. "Trust me, Earthling, it was the only way."

"And now you're here to anal probe me and dissect my bloody carcass," I said, mustering as much indignation as possible. Which was very little, given that he was a superior being and I was nearly naked in my back yard, my only gun of the water variety.

Thankfully, his smile returned. "No, just to study your sexual behavior. I wish to learn if our similarities run merely skin deep."

I echoed his smile with one of my own. "I don't know," I said, seductively adding, "You're not really showing all that much skin, deep or otherwise." He responded by reaching for the zipper at the top of his suit. I quickly stopped him. "Wait!" I shouted. "Please, it's bad enough that your ship is in my backyard; adding a naked alien to the mix is sure to bring out a team of unruly *National Inquirer* reporters."

He pressed a button on his lapel. The ship shimmered and vanished. He strode into my house with me close behind. "Better?" he asked.

"Almost," I said, reaching for the zipper and gliding it down. I parted the suit and slid it around his shoulders, revealing a finely toned chest and rock-solid abs, all covered in a thick, brown down. Again he reached for my robe, this time dropping it to the floor. My hands instinctively roamed his torso. His did the same to mine.

"Well, top part's identical," I made note.

"Yes, Earthling, but I'm afraid the bottom is quite different."

I gulped. "Different? Please tell me you have male sexual organs tucked away in there."

His eyes, blue as the sky he emerged from, twinkled. He looked down at my rod, which was already engorged and throbbing, and held it in his hand, sending a warm flush through my crotch and down my now shaking legs. "Yes," he said. "Like you, my sexual organs are of the male variation." He confirmed this by slipping his hands into his suit and yanking it down to the ground. "But we, you see, have two to your one."

I sucked in my breath as my eyes landed on both of his cocks, each of which was already growing, thickening, widening, inch by steady inch, until they were jutting out from his magnificent hirsute body a good eight fat ones, one pointing eastward, the other west.

"There's an old Earth saying," I quipped, once I regained my senses. "It goes: two heads are better than one."

He took both of his hands and stroked both of his dicks as he explained. "Our scientists believe we evolved with two sexual organs in order to allow for multiple partners, which in turn allows for multiple pregnancies. More pregnancies mean more offspring. Survival of the species. Except that we no longer have offspring. Instead, we clone ourselves as need be, always keeping the population at a steady level. And now we only have sex for the enjoyment of it."

I reached down and began a slow stroke on my measly single peter. "Ironically, on this planet, my kind pretty much only have sex for the enjoyment of it, too."

"Your kind?" he asked, again tilting his head like a confused puppy.

"Homo-*homo sapiens*. In other words, a human male that only makes it with other males."

"Ah, I see. We do not practice this on my planet. May I watch you do this and learn from you?"

I looked down at both of his massive schlongs and thought of my one tight hole. Then I glanced up and caught sight of the hunky, naked Hans across the way. "Two cocks, two holes," I whispered. I wasn't even sure that he would be interested in either, but figured it was worth a shot to find out, for interplanetary peace and all. And in the interest of science. Not to mention that both guys were super hot and I was super horny by that point.

So I put my robe back on and, handing my alien friend one from the bathroom closet, I grabbed his hand in mine and headed him over to my neighbor's house. I knocked on his door and waited.

Hans answered by poking his handsome head out. "Yes, may I help you?" he asked in a sexy, thick accent that dripped of Octoberfest and schnitzel.

I was clearly in uncharted territory and decided that honesty would probably be best. "Um, yeah. Um, hi, Hans. I'm Luke, your next-door neighbor. And this is, this is…"

"Spandex," the alien informed.

I looked at him. "Really?" He nodded, unconcerned. I turned back to Hans. Yes. Spandex. He's one of the aliens and he wants to watch us have sex." To which I quickly added, "For the sake of alien science, of course."

Hans's jaw dropped only slightly. "This is American joke, yes? Perhaps that show *Punk'd* I watch on reruns."

I opened my robe for him, my cock already beginning its gradual lift. "No joke," I said.

Spandex followed suit and opened his robe. "No joke," he added.

The jaw dropped entirely as Hans's eyes went from my hard-on to the alien's, both of them. Then he opened the door to reveal his magnificent naked glory. "For science!" he said, a mischievous smirk spreading across his handsome stubbled faced. "Please, come in."

Of course, all I heard was that "come" part.

Hans closed the door behind us. We dropped our robes and the three of us stood there, naked, and, a mere few seconds later, hard.

"Commence," the alien commanded.

We, of course, obeyed. Gladly. I wrapped my hands around Hans's thin waist and pulled him toward me. His soft lips were on mine in a flash as his deft tongue found my own. Our cocks pressed up against our bellies and our hands roamed each other's backs and rumps as we made out in front of the ogling alien. Truly, it was voyeurism of the oddest kind.

"Interesting," we heard him say. "On my planet, we do not do this thing you are doing with your mouths."

I separated my lips from Hans's, still pressing my body tight up against him. "It's called kissing. Here, try it," I offered.

Spandex walked over and slowly inched his head toward mine. Tentatively, he placed his lips on my lips. I frenched him as the German stroked the head of my cock. The alien moaned in delight and moved to my neighbor's eager mouth. I joined the both of them, three mouths sucking and slurping and swapping some heavy spit as four cocks were stroked and tugged, slathered in precome.

"That is quite enjoyable," Spandex soon said with a heavy sigh. "We only use this orifice for eating."

I grinned at Hans. "Then stand back and watch what else it can do."

I dropped to my knees to take a deep draw on the head of my neighbor's slick willy. He smelled of sweat and musk, a heady aroma that drew me in and around and down. I tugged on his hefty, hairy balls as I worked his tool down my throat. The German bucked his ass, sending his fat rod in and back. I gagged, but managed to engulf all seven meaty inches as a tear streamed down my cheek.

Hans groaned and winked at the alien. "You'd like to try this, too?"

Spandex nodded in rapt wonder as Hans grabbed my head and shoved it onto one of the alien's massive cocks. He fell to his knees and joined me on the floor, beginning a slow, steady suck on its twin, until we were both in sync. We deep-throated the matching set while Spandex pumped our faces, the German and I fiddling with each other's assholes from behind our backs.

"Oh yes," the alien moaned. "I guess my kind is not as advanced as I once thought." He petted the tops of our heads and asked, "What else can your mouths do?"

I prodded further into my neighbor's hole. He quickly took the hint, popping the cock out of his mouth and getting on all fours. I released cock number two and turned to Hans's upturned, perfect ass. I slapped each cheek in turn, the sound pinging in the small entryway, before spreading him apart to reveal a hair-rimmed, crinkled ring which winked out at me, all come-hither-like. "Nice," I whispered, delving around and then deeper inside with my tongue, lapping eagerly at his silky man-hole.

"Nice," Hans echoed, pushing his ass into my face before inviting the alien to join us.

Spandex crouched down and got on all fours as well, so that Hans could eat out the alien's ass while he in turn ate out mine, until the three of us formed an ass-munching triangle. "Nice," Spandex groaned into my hole, thereby making it unanimous. "I did not know that an anus could be used for sexual gratification."

Hans laughed and slipped a wet finger up the alien's hairy rump. "No?" he asked. "How is this for sexual gratification then?" One finger quickly became two, both of which reached in and back and began a slow fuck up Spandex's stunningly beautiful rear end.

"Oh," the alien moaned, deep and low and rumbling, like a runaway freight car. "Oh, yes. Yes, that feels very nice."

He apparently felt like sharing the wealth because a second later I felt two slender fingers entering my own ass, both of them finding just the right depth and speed to send my cock into pulsing overdrive. Naturally, I returned the favor, fingering Hans's tight hole with not two but three spit-slick digits, until all three of us were bucking and groaning on the floor, our asses mercilessly worked, our cocks flopping between our parted legs.

Spandex was panting faster now. I wondered if he was close. If he was, I didn't want him to come just yet. "Switch," I said.

"Switch?" the alien asked. "Into what? This is my only form."

I laughed. "No, I mean, switch positions."

I popped my fingers out of Hans's ass. We all hopped up and moved in toward each other, our bodies meshed into a stroking, caressing, grabbing entanglement, until it was impossible to tell where one of us ended and the other began.

Spandex sunk to his knees. We gazed down at him as he stared longingly at our cocks. "One has more skin on the end than the other one," he said, a note of curiosity to his voice.

I didn't want to go into the drawn out details of how sometimes we humans practice odd ancient rituals, and so instead I said, "It's colder in Germany, so my friend here needs a sort of sweater."

"Turtleneck sweater," amended my neighbor with an endearing giggle.

Spandex nodded. I wondered how his field report was going to read. "Makes sense."

It did? I shrugged. *Fine by me.* Finer when he began to suck my cock while stroking Hans's, his mouth surprisingly adept, considering he was a blowing neophyte. Up and down he went on my pole. In and out my cock appeared and disappeared, as a million volts of adrenaline shot up my spine and a bead of sweat meandered its way down my chest.

Out popped my prick. In went Hans's. Spandex's mouth was replaced by a hand. My balls bounced as the alien jacked me.

I turned to Hans and grinned. "You know, I watch you walk around your house naked," I told him.

The smile rose northward on his face. "I know. It's why I walk around the house naked."

Both our cocks miraculously found their way down Spandex's throat at the exact same time. Chalk one up to evolutionary supremacy.

"Switch," Spandex eventually said, his breath now ragged and raspy.

"What position would you like now?" I asked, eager to please our Earthly visitor.

Spandex's mouth shrugged, but then his eyes again sparkled and he held up his finger. It must've been a universal sign for: *I've got a great idea!* "Would you Earthlings like to go for a ride on my sexual organs?"

Music to my ears.

And Hans's, apparently. He rushed out and back with two rubbers and a jar of Wet. The alien lay down on the ground, staring in confused amusement as my neighbor worked the condoms down both of his pricks before lubing them up. *Are the rubbers necessary?* I wondered. Then again, lord only knew what microbes the alien brought with him from deep space, and I for one was none too eager to wake up with a new kind of STD, like one that caused meteor-sized protrusions on my rather fetching nether regions.

In any case, I quickly straddled Spandex's right leg and Hans his left, the two of us facing the Matt-Lauer-like alien before us. Like magnets, three pairs of lips again found one another as we slowly squatted down, our assholes pressed snugly above the alien's cock heads. We pushed our rumps and allowed the intrusion, causing a flush of warmth to spread from my ass to my belly. My already fat cock swelled and throbbed and bounced.

I opened my eyes to see a look of pure ecstasy spread across my neighbor's face. "One small step for man..." he whispered into my ear, taking my lobe between his teeth for a nibble.

"Two giant cocks for our kind," I finished the thought, reaching out to stroke Hans's hooded cock, which was already leaking copious amounts of precome. I licked my sticky fingers as I raised and lowered my ass down on Spandex's massive second prick. Soon enough, the German and I were riding in tandem, filling the area around us with the sound of our rather loud grunts and groans.

"I am close," the alien eventually proclaimed, shoving his dicks to the hilts. Both Hans and I stroked our cocks faster, until we both tossed our heads back in unison. With deep, long sighs, we shot mammoth loads of hot, white, sticky come that landed on our new friend. Beneath us, Spandex filled the rubbers—and our asses—with his own hefty loads.

Panting, we both looked down at the alien, who was grinning as he wiped the sweat from his creaseless brow with one hand, sliding his other through the dripping remains of our interplanetary three-way. "So," he finally said. "Have you Earthlings ever been to Africa? It really is beautiful this time of year. And wait until you see the giraffes!"

I looked at the two of them and laughed. "U.F.O.," I said.

"Huh?" Hans popped Spandex's prick out of his ass.

"Unbelievable fucking offer," I informed, following suit.

Spandex echoed my laughter. "So, will you take it?" he asked.

"Who can turn down giraffes?"

"And double-dicked aliens," Hans added, and rightly so.

Spandex beamed and, much to our delight, both his mammoth cocks started to swell and jut straight up again.

"Good," he said, reaching up to pet our still-throbbing holes. "Then I think it's time for another invasion."

"Invade away," I said, getting on all fours before spreading my cheeks for him. "Invade the fuck away."

SEA GLASS
ROBERT RUSSIN

The light burned and blinded. I could never have survived up there. It could never have lasted. I need to remind myself of that, when my mind flits away from these hard truths and tries to cradle itself in softer, prettier lies. There are terrible things down here in the dark, and the temptation to dream of a way out is stronger than my self restraint.

But still, I need to remain alert.

I've been alive long enough—too long—and I know how to blend into the rock, to hide from things that would devour me. Nothing hunts with greater tenacity, nothing more capable of destructive hunger than the idle mind; there's not much to occupy it beneath the waves. Body and brain dwell in the dark, dwell in the past. Memory is a coral reef, living and changeable with too many places for things to hide. Its corners are jagged, brittle, abrasive. Surprisingly fragile. The salt in the sea is corrosive to these sharper edges of recollection. It erodes and softens pain into something that is, if not pleasure, at least something smoothed to a dull, throbbing ache. Polished, reflective, deceptive.

Memory becomes sea glass, a false treasure. I see past the pain and past the endless dark and in the trick of the false light I see only your blue eyes staring back at me.

I'm a broken thing now, scorched and twisted. I don't know how old I am. Existence in the deepest depths stretches out endless and infinite. I know it would have been better to burn and freeze and explode in that one frenzied night, letting the pieces of myself scatter to the wind and the stars, than to linger down here forever poisoned with its memory. But I'm a coward, with no taste for heroic ends. So I float on, and try to forget.

The coast of Provincetown is a harsh cradle, and only certain things can survive its churning chaos long enough to call it home. We're wave-pounded and rock-pounded and we don't have the luxury of tender soft skin to beat against its hard stones. This ocean doesn't coddle its poor chitinous children—the world down here is harsh and hard and we grow harsher and harder to shield ourselves from these rough and rocky shores.

There is life down here, of course. Life has an innate stubbornness in its persistence to thrive where it shouldn't. Those of us that survived here did so by growing shells, growing sharp, growing into the rock. We lack the flash and finery of our colorful kinfolk in calmer, gentler waters. You won't see bright orange fins or beautiful trailing ornamental designs on our bodies. No children would be delighted to look into a glass and see us staring back. We are grey and steel and grit and teeth—hard shells, soft, oozing innards. I suppose you'd call my kind the dominant species down here, though we mostly keep to ourselves these days. We have always been here, lurking, watching. There are not as many of us as there once were, and this is probably for the best. We're hatched things. We know no mother, no gentle touch beyond the caress of our own dark dreams.

Sometimes over the course of an endless life we seek temporary companionship. I've heard rumors, in passing, of an ancient underwater city where some of us skulk away the centuries, but I've never sought it out. I can't imagine any world my kind built together being anything other than a nightmare.

We stay out of sight, which is lucky for anything with eyes because we're not something you'd want to see down in the dark. We could end the world above should the desire strike us, but we have neither motive nor inclination. We live in a different world, and the less I say about it the better. It's not a pretty one.

I'm alone here now, by choice as well as necessity. I came back altered. The stench of humanity is underneath my skin, and the rest of my kind would probably see me as food before they saw me as a companion. Above all else: survival. I might even be able to say we've turned it into an art form if any of us had any of the gentler parts of sentience that would allow us to make art. We eat, we shit, we fuck in a mindless, pleasureless way to propagate a species which existed long before anything above the surface shed its hair and walked upright.

But enough about us. This is an account of love, of lust, of passion.

Those of us that remain beneath the waves are anathema to these nobler sentiments, knowing nothing but blind, stupid hunger. I was no different. So what happened to me?

It was you. It was all you. It's you I will spend my endless empty days and maddening lonely nights trying to forget. It's you who taught me to surrender to pleasure, to embrace pain. It's you who gave me a tantalising taste of a better life. Ruthless. It's you who changed me into this.

I want to forget. I won't forget. I can't forget.

Most of the time, I can drift on the currents and dream in the dark. It hurts most when the moon is full. The moon is what pulled me to you, out of the sea and into your arms. Moonlight is what framed you, and how I see your face. Moonlight was the backdrop of our dance together, moonlight is how I remember you. A pale, shimmering false light replete with falser promises.

It pulls me to the surface, pulls the memories out from the corners of my shattered mind, pulls me in a way I still don't understand, and when I burn my weak and bulbous eyes with its silver light I'm brought back there again, a tenth time, a hundredth time.

I was asleep. I have no way of measuring or counting the endless years through which I slept. Time is something different down here. We don't fear it or try to outrun it like you do in the crazy chaos above the waves. We float beside it, weave in and out of it, sleep in its embrace. We drift with something resembling awareness of it but its passing means nothing.

I still don't understand how it happened. In the deepest, darkest parts of the sea, I dreamed a dark dream. Something in you called to me. I woke up. Through the empty fathoms, my body answered. Unable to stop myself, I swam to the surface to meet the daylight, something I don't remember ever doing in my long life. It was too bright, too harsh, too loud, this world above the waves. Fire and knives and noise, unbearable. My eyes burned. I was blind. I saw nothing but white glare. But I heard you. I felt you. And through the searing heat and agony, I saw a pair of eyes that cast a calm blue ocean over all the pain.

I could do nothing to reach you. I sank below and waited for the sun to do the same. When it was gone, so were you. There was no moon that night, but I didn't need one. That half imagined glimpse of your eyes cast enough light to see down into the deepest depths of my abyssal hell. I found it lacking.

My body started changing in ways I didn't understand. I became heavier, ungainly in the water. Softer. Every night I returned, my desire for you growing and swelling as the moon above me did the same. Sometimes, I'd imagine that I could see you and the man that was beside you, walking near the shore, sitting by the bay. Sometimes I thought I heard echoes of you and him, laughter—that tinkling golden sound, so alien to my ears accustomed to nothing but the roar of the waves and the silence of the deep. But I was never certain if any of this was real or just fevered hallucinations brought on by my aching need for you.

I'm an underwater thing, blind to everything except my own mindless stupid cellular needs, monstrous even to myself. A cold and shapeless ball of fat and claws and teeth. There are others; we are hideous to one another as well. I've never wanted them. I've never wanted any of this.

The moon is large in the sky tonight and suddenly I'm there and it's happening to me again.

I see him first, the man that you love. He is walking along the silver shore, enjoying the sea air in the moonlight. In that world that is not mine, can't be mine, can never be mine, I see him. He's a cold presence, something familiar—a hunter like me. I find myself comforted by him.

But then you appear from the house by the shore, and my blood turns hot and starts to boil. You take his hand. It's the two of you; you walk together, talk together, love together, creatures of the golden dawn that I can never touch. The pull of your love and the pull of the moon and the pull of my aching emptiness are too much and it feels as if I will burst if I don't rip my skin off.

Maybe you found the night air disagreeable, because you're suddenly gone, and he's alone again, and so am I, and I can't bear to be alone. I need him. I need you. I need to follow you. I will follow you anywhere.

I think of nothing else.

The moonlight is too bright, too harsh. I hate myself. I look at my grey skin; rubbery folds of fat to keep me warm beneath the waves of the harsh north sea. I dream of your tight, solid skin over bones so hard, so strong. I need you. I feel nothing. I can no longer see in the dark, my blind translucent eyes see only you. Only you.

My body is a pale sickly moon, rising weighted and bloated over the bay, swollen with lust and with need for you. It's a pain I've never known and it's deep inside of me. My cold, necrotic skin is about to burst, to explode with the maggots of desire feeding and getting fat on the need I have for you deep within my heart.

I take a gnarled bone claw and puncture a fold of grey glutinous flesh—hard rubbery folds, too many layers between you and my pulsing beating heart or what I assume is my heart. A hot stink hisses out and dissipates, losing its putrescent self in the night wind. Pain and relief, but not enough. I tear the hole wider, slitting my way through fat and grease and bile, and slide out of my blubbery skin and I'm cold, I'm gasping, I'm naked on the shore.

It's unbearable, this zephyr, this noise, this dry cold screaming of the wind on this fickle changeable world after a millennia spent in the constancy of the waves that cradled me. I'm choking, I'm dying. This world is too cold, too hard. Too undecided. The wind's slightest change feels like a thousand little knives against my new skin. How do people live like this, without the constant weight of the water to hold them? I feel lost, drifting and exposed.

⚘

He comes to me first, and helps me to my new unsteady feet. Of course it is he who found me. Like me, he is a hunter, a predator. He's got the sharper eyes, the hungrier eyes. I see a cold and kindred spirit in him. He asks me if I'm drunk. I answer instinctively with a voice that sounds alien, dry, crackling to my ears still deafened by the slicing, shrieking wind. *Dry*, I say. *Need water*. I itch and claw at my skin.

He walks me with my wobbling, useless legs to a wooden structure behind the house, open to the sky and that enormous staring moon, and sits me on a bench. An outdoor shower. He turns a knob and warm water shoots from above. My skin drinks it desperately. I stop shivering and begin to relax.

He grabs me by the neck and shoves his tongue into my mouth. A cold hand, a cold tongue, an eel wriggling its way into a small cave. My first instinct is to bite it off but I hold back and give into it and find that it feels good. Hands grab the back of my throbbing head and I begin to understand why I clawed my way out from the sea.

And then you're there, and my world is destroyed. I've had an ugly life and have never seen true beauty until this moment. I don't understand your words but I feel them, feel the heat of your breath, your skin. You've absorbed the sun's heat and the sun's light that I couldn't bear and you beam it back at me like the moon's gentle glow. It burns away the last lingering parts of the underwater thing I used to be. I can never go back from here. I don't want to go back from here.

I'm cold, still. I run the back of my new hand over your beard. It's soft, it's thick, it's strange and wonderful to a cold hairless thing like me and I can't handle it yet. I fall down to my knees and kneel in front of you. I shiver as I stare at you, and wonder what your blue eyes see when they look down at me, this strange new form I have. You are beautiful. In this moment when you stand above me, the shower spray cascading over your hard, hairy body, you are a sea god and I know I will worship you until the day I die.

You look down into my eyes, and you touch my face with one hand, yourself with the other. You start to piss on me now. All over my new body and my face, bathing me with that warm golden glow of the memory of sunlight, summer's dandelion wine. I open my mouth and drink it, growing stronger, growing warmer as it runs down my throat. Your stream is endless and it spills all over me and I'm finally warm. I drink in the sunshine. I let the echo of a summer I will never know wash all over me, getting drunk from it, getting hard from it, and I put my mouth on you and swallow every last drop of it. My blood is hot now, my body on fire. I am strong.

You both work together as a team. You've done this before but I don't care. I discover the joys of the body, the joys of touch. I'm delighted to find that the twin little barnacles on my chest are sensitive. I have two mouths on me, sucking and biting gently, two remoras nibbling at me as four hands brush across the uncharted parts of this new body, fingers spreading out and tickling like I'm floating through an underwater forest of kelp, bringing me just to the edge of pain and madness. I scream with a voice that sounds shrill and gurgling rising up through the warm water to emerge into the night air.

He doesn't seem to like my wailing. He covers my mouth and slaps me in the face. I moan and push against him but I'm not used to this body yet and he forces me back against the wall. He slaps me again; his cold hand on my hot stinging cheek is sharp but not unpleasant. He grabs my throat, pushing my head back into the wall, and squeezes. *Shut the fuck up*, he says to me, as I choke and gasp and my body burns and wants him to hit it again.

The steam of the water, the wood of the wall: this is the only way we could have met, this marriage between earth and sea. He's a tempest, throwing me around easily and carelessly. I'm a gull, caught in his cold sea swell which shows no mercy, and I beat my useless wings furiously against his rage but find myself helpless to fly against it. I can't fight it or save myself from drowning as he batters me like the cold wind and waves.

He's biting me and choking me and it's all okay. Through the chaos, all throughout this storm I lock eyes with you. I gaze into two limpid pools of the most beautiful blue I've ever seen, blue that makes me think of calm tropical seas and I feel safe, I feel loved, I find a gentle calm in the midst of this gale that batters me.

Your hands, so caring, so warm, spread my legs, slowly, softly, and you teach me about a pleasure and a need I could never imagine as your mouth finds its way home. Your tongue is fat, your tongue is hot, and you flick it, lightly, the slightest fluttering of a guppy's fin, and I groan and cry out and force my screams against his cold hands still around my neck and over my mouth. I'm safe, I'm okay. I see past this pain and fury into the blue ocean between my legs.

I feel stronger, but I'm not yet ready for what your tongue is making my body want. You're making me aware of my emptiness but I'm not ready to be filled. I need to move, to see what this new body can do. I turn around and with new strength I slam him into the bench. I find his hole with my own tongue and taste. There's sweat, there's salt, and it tastes like the sea. As it puckers and gapes and swallows my mouth, I feel certain if I press my ear to it I will hear the ocean, echoing through him. He's cold and empty, a dead and vacant shell. I'm a hermit crab looking for a home. I need to fill him.

I stand. You gasp. I look down. I look different from you and him. Where your thick, solid appendage is I have a long and writhing tentacle, with a gaping sucking mouth of its own. I guess I didn't get this entirely right. It doesn't matter now; it's got a mind of its own and it finds its way into his little throbbing scallop and plunges in.

For the first time, I'm linked with another being, and it's wonderful, though it still seems entirely out of my control. Whatever has grown between my legs is taking me along with it, carrying me and pulling me and slamming my hips into him as it sucks and searches the dark and empty cavern of his cold body.

It's almost too much. I'm on the verge of rocketing off of this cold dying rock and out into the infinity of the endless black ocean above us, but you hold me. You anchor me to a warm safe place, and I thrust against him as my tentacular arm writhes and sucks and gasps and grasps for the little spot inside of him that's making him scream. I'm feeling him squeeze against me and milk me and it's too much and I shoot, for the first time, my hot milt into him, gallons of it, spilling out, covering all of us as he screams and slams his head against the wood boards and squeezes me so tight that I think it's about to rip this part off of me. It smells like low tide.

I feel the tentacle retreating, feel it coming back to me. His body twitches and we both retract into ourselves. My legs are weak; I fall onto the floor. The tide recedes without me. I'd be left gasping for air, but you catch me. Of course you catch me. I feel as if you'd always catch me, for all eternity, if you could only come beneath the waves with me. You'd never let me sink or fall again. I am caught forever in those two blue tidal pools, those beautiful blue eyes. I am reflected back, lost, searching for a home and finding one. For the rest of my life I will be stuck in that beautiful pool, drowning but never dying, a slave to those azure orbs.

As my breathing slows, you stand and let me taste you, his cold arms still wrapped around me, your hot hands on the back of my head. You're guiding yourself into my mouth, forcing yourself in. It's hot and thick and almost burns. The sweetest salty drops of the sweetest salty sea drip from you—nothing will ever taste this sweet again.

I'm choking and I don't care. It's too big for my tiny mouth and my eyes are tearing as it tries to find its way down my throat, thick and engorged with blood and unable to fit. For the first time, I know total surrender. After spending a thousand mindless years fighting currents, fighting tides, fighting to keep myself afloat, I learn the liberation that comes from the cessation of struggle, of resistance. I learn the freedom of total servitude. It's a beautiful death, this letting go. Your hips rock faster and I'm choking and I'm gagging and heaving and I'm giving my entire body and my entire heart over to you, and then I feel that I'm ready. I have no more decisions to make. My body is yours. Everything inside it is yours. Take it.

He holds my legs back, his grip cold and firm on my burning inner thighs, and you're on the floor. I let the current take me, let go completely; I'm yours.

Your tongue finds that spot between my legs and my entire body starts to writhe. You run it all around and softly start to let it work its way in, gentle waves in the bay lapping lightly on the shore. I'm screaming and this time he doesn't stop me. This is something I never understood, how it feels this good to be taken, to stop fighting, to be owned, after drifting alone in an endless dark ocean for so long. I don't know or care if it's sweat or tears or the ocean in my eyes, and I throw my head back and look up and see the moonlight scattered in the shower spray, bright and blinding white light like the passage into death.

And then with one hand you pull my head forward, and you kiss me, and my body relaxes. That little cave you discovered opens, opens wider than the gulf between sea and sky, and your eyes stare into mine. I know I'm yours forever, no matter the hurt, no matter the pain, no matter that you already belong to the man with the cold hands pulling my legs back behind my head and sucking on my toes.

I'm lying there, wide open, and with my head thrown back I see you lean across me and kiss him, your husband, and I feel that I'm the bridge between the two of you, a conduit for your love. I have no will of my own and no purpose but to offer up my body for you both, a tribute to the two of you together. After fighting alone for so long, I need you both to take me and do whatever the fuck you want with me.

The little space between my legs is hungry, and somehow it stretches and beckons—you don't force your way in, it pulls you in, like the moon pulled me to you. Its hunger generates its own tide, its own gravitational energy; it opens so much wider than I thought it could and swallows your entire cock. I never thought you'd be able to fit inside but it just barely manages to take all of you. You gasp as you slide all the way in to the top of your balls, as full and low and heavy as the swollen moon. You gasp and lose control for just a second, pitch forward. Your hot breath in my ear makes me shiver. You whisper, "I love you."

These words more than anything set my tentacle flailing again and I watch it dance in its blind mindless hunger as you start to pound into me, ramming me with your thick cock and crashing into me like a gigantic tidal swell. It pounds me angrily—wet, furious, like hurricane waves on a helpless shore filling and flooding and devastating, obliterating. You're massive and thick and swollen and every space inside of me is stretched and filled and about to be ripped to shreds. He is hard again and he straddles me now and shoves himself into my mouth to stop me from screaming and waking up the entire town. It sounds like I'm being murdered and I don't care because in a way I am; this little death is bringing forth a new version of me, one that was always meant to be.

I'm filled so deep, so completely, and four hands run across my body, pinching and slapping and hitting and grabbing. All I feel are two furious bodies, one hot and one cold, doing to me what a storm does to a beach. You're looking down at me and the look in your eyes is as hungry and desperate and furious and loving and needing and lonely as mine. I see you and I see me and I see our entire lives as we lock eyes and this moment is perfect and right and oh my god you're pounding me so hard I can't stop... I'm exploding all over myself, shooting hot sticky thick juice everywhere. Two sharks turn me into useless meat and rip me apart. I'm drowning and dying in this ocean of blood.

You spit on my face and slap me, and the wet smack sounds like something breaking the surface of the sea; it sounds like a breaking heart because I know this won't last forever.

You pull out and the immediate emptiness I feel is overshadowed when you take my head and shove yourself back into my mouth. You shoot down my throat, hot and salty like the sea. It tastes like home.

I'm still drowning—drowning in love, drowning in honey and in sweetness, and for the rest of my life everything that's not you will turn to dust and ash, filth and rot, in my mouth.

I try to look at you, try to feel your heat, but you're already cooling. The fire is fading. The embers are dying. The sky is growing lighter, and already you're evaporating, a dew drop vanishing with the coming dawn. My body twitches, still wet, still reeling from the storm of you.

There is so much still to explore in the depths of this sea, the three of our bodies able to form infinite patterns of pleasure in the currents of our pulsing blood. We could have lived wildly, lived in love, every night exploring the depths of what we could make each other feel.

But you're already gone.

⚜

I DON'T REMEMBER how I got back to the sea. I have a vague recollection of the sun's first weak rays rising over the wood beams, of burning my new skin. Blind, crippled, trembling. I somehow must have dragged my hideous twisted body back to the bay to sink beneath the waves. I'm broken now, no longer entirely a creature of the deep but unable to live above the waves, so I float in an empty stasis, dreaming and aching..

You've marked me, changed me forever into something that's both more beautiful and more hideous than I ever thought I could be. I float around, avoid my own kind. They wouldn't recognize me in my current state. I burn and long to be taken, to be filled again, but I know I will never be able to give myself over the way I did to you.

Once a month, when the moon is full, I drift to the surface and remember. I see it there, as cold and distant and beautiful and shining with false light as you, equally unreachable. I talk to you, hoping that somewhere, in some part of this cold and broken world, the moon will beam these words to you and you'll hear them in your sleep—maybe dream of my voice or of my arms or of my eyes or of my mouth, and how I love you, how I need you.

But I was just a tiny pebble dropped into your pond, causing tiny ripples that meant nothing, already forgotten. You yourself were as much a creature of the deep as me, using tricks and false light to lure the blind and the stupid into death.

Back home beneath the waves, there is one small mercy—I cannot cry. With my nightmare bulbous monster eyes, I peer unblinking into the empty darkness of the deep. If my eyes seem swollen, it's a mere accident of my unfortunate form. The sea cradles me again, an entire ocean of salt tears. I taste you in every drop of this infinity.

I'm yours, for the rest of my miserable days. Find me when the moon is full.

STRAWBERRIES
JERRY L. WHEELER

The young man bit into the flesh of the small end. Wrapping his lips around its firmness, he sucked slightly as a thin runner of red juice trickled into his scraggly blond beard. He lifted the hem of his grimy t-shirt and wiped his mouth, showing off a thick treasure trail that distracted the hell out of Kyle. He smiled while he chewed, seeds sticking to his teeth. "How much?" he asked.

Kyle shrugged with studied casualness and—for no reason other than effect—looked at the gold Rolex strapped to his wrist. He wasn't one of the company's top negotiators for nothing. He shaded his eyes against the sun as he surveyed a large, verdant space between two dusty construction sites bordered by high chain link fencing. "I dunno. Three fifty an acre. Maybe four hundred."

The farmer chuckled low and pitched the remainder of the strawberry over Kyle's head. It landed somewhere in the corn stalks on the other side of the road. He reached up and grabbed the bottom edge of the sign over the stand. It read *Farmer Howie's Produce*. "Man, I've been made lowball offers before," he said, "but that was the lowest and took the most balls to make."

He let go of the sign and hooked his long, spade shaped thumbs into the empty belt loops of his low-slung jeans. Kyle could see the sweat soaked waistband of his Joe Boxers. With the Chinese symbol tats on his biceps, his faint case of acne and a pierced tongue, he looked more like a sagger sk8r dude than a farmer.

He ran a hand over his buzzed blonde hair. "No offense, man, but your offer's a fuckin' joke. You need my land to connect up these two malls, and it ain't gonna happen. It's not for sale."

"Everything's for sale. I just haven't found your price yet."

"*No* price, dude," Farmer Howie insisted. "Why would I wanna give this up? Land's blessed." He swept his arm around the field. "Look at those tomatoes, look at that corn." Reaching back to the produce stand, he plucked a strawberry from its box. "Check out these berries, man—sweetest you ever tasted." He held it out for Kyle.

"Can't. I'm allergic." He cast his eyes over the land again, with its tall rows of corn and flat expanses of strawberries as he drank in the earthy scent of tomatoes ripening under the watchful gaze of two scarecrows propped high among the corn silk tassels. Kyle stared purposefully into the farmer's nut-brown eyes, trying to discern any trace of guile, but all he saw was his own. "I'll double my offer, then," he said. "Eight hundred. Maybe I can even get my company to go for nine."

"Nope," Farmer Howie replied. "Not for sale." He reached his hand under his shirt and scratched his chest, exposing a swath of tan skin and a patch of downy blonde hair between his pecs. Kyle couldn't think of anything else to say. All he could do was stare at the farmer's half naked chest, wondering what he looked like with his shirt off. And wondering how to find out. When he raised his eyes, Farmer Howie was grinning at him.

Kyle's voice shook. "How many acres are we talking about, here?"

The front of his shirt dropped down again as Farmer Howie brought his hand to his eyes and gazed into the distance. "About two-fifty on both sides of the road."

"Five hundred acres. Look, if I can get my company to go a thousand an acre, you're lookin' at half a million in your pocket. Not a bad piece of change."

Farmer Howie grabbed three tomatoes from the farthest bin and began to juggle them. "Big money means big headaches. Don't need it. Got my little house up the road, produce stand makin' some money. I do all right. Sorry, dude. It's not for sale."

The juggling action dropped his sagging jeans even lower, dangerously close to his pubic line. Kyle thought he saw a few tufts of dark blonde hair peeking out of the Joe Boxers. Or was it his imagination? "Let me talk to my company and see what I can do. I'll be back tomorrow."

"Whenever," the farmer said. "It still ain't gonna be for sale." He stopped juggling and tossed one of the tomatoes to Kyle. "Here" he said, "on the house. Best damn tomato you ever ate. Land's blessed, I tell ya."

Kyle caught it with one hand. Even though it had been in the shade of the stand, it felt warm. Almost as if it had been alive.

❦

"Okay, Leo – okay, I *get* it already." He jabbed at his phone, flipped it shut and threw it across the seat. Fuckin' dickwad, he thought. Like I don't already know how important this deal is. Like I don't already know about the two guys who fucked it up and were so embarrassed they never even came back to work. Like I don't already know I'm out on my ass if I can't make this happen. Does he think the goddamn pressure *helps?*

Kyle pulled into the parking lot of the Sand and Surf, a rundown motel whose name was wishful prairie thinking, being five hundred miles from the nearest body of water. Despite its landlocked condition, ocean waves of blue neon washed over the "Vacancy" sign. This looks like as good a place to spend the night as any, Kyle thought. Fact is, it looks like the *only* place.

He opened the door and stepped down onto the dusty, weed-dotted pavement, reaching back into his Explorer for his New York Yankees baseball cap. He settled the cap on his head and trudged up a cracked sidewalk bordered by spindly yellow tea roses. A string of bells jangled against the door as he opened it, but no one appeared at the tiny counter in the lobby.

The moist breeze from a swamp cooler brushed Kyle's cheek and he smelled bacon frying. A sitcom laugh track brayed from a television somewhere in the room behind the counter. He hit the bell on the desk a few times. "Hello?" he ventured. "Anyone here?"

The query produced some shuffling from the inner room. A scruffy grey cat bounded out, followed by a large, tired-looking woman with orange hair and too much makeup. Her mottled red and white arms plumped out of her sleeveless daisy print housedress like summer sausages, and she gripped a greasy fork. Kyle heard her breathing from across the room.

"You lost?" she asked.

"Just passing through on business," he said. "Any rooms available?"

"Twenty-six rooms, twenty-six vacancies. 'Course the new shopping center they're buildin' up the road might change that." She scratched her nose and put the fork down on the counter, turning the guest register towards him. "That the business you're here on?"

"Yep." He fished a business card out of his wallet and handed it to her, letting her read it as he signed the register. The two most recent names had been whited out. After a momentary hesitation, he signed over one of them. "Kyle Arbogast, Armbruster Development. What can you tell me about the farmer who runs the produce stand up the road?"

"Howie? Not much to tell." She whirled the guest book back around and looked at it hastily before getting a key from the board behind her. "Used to be a ski bum in Colorado. He came back here a few years ago to run the farm after his granddaddy died. But if you're lookin' to buy that land of his, you can forget it."

"Why?"

"He won't never sell it. That's what I told those other two."

"What about the other two?"

"BEATRICE, WHERE'S MY SUPPAH?" came a scream from the back room.

"S'cuse me," she said, handing him the key. "I got to finish gettin' Daddy's supper. You're in room twelve—far end of the unit so's you won't hear our television or nothin'. Nearest cafe's in Taylorville about ten miles up the road, but they also got a pizza place that delivers out here. Just call if you need somethin.'" Grabbing the fork off the counter, she licked at the congealing grease and disappeared into the back room followed by the cat.

Kyle picked up his suitcase and found his room at the end of the unit. The door stuck, so he put his shoulder to it and pushed. A wave of hot stale air greeted him. He threw the window open and turned on the swamp cooler. I'll just dump the bag and get something to eat in town, he thought.

He threw his suitcase on the bed, but it bounced off and landed on the other side of the bed near the bathroom. As he bent over to pick it up, he saw something shiny on the floor poking out from the bedspread fringe. A cell phone. A cell phone just like his, right down to the label that read "Property of

Armbruster Development." He sat his laptop up on the desk and plugged the phone in.

Jack Dumont had five messages, but Kyle couldn't pick them up without his password. Probably from Leo anyway, he thought. No text messages, but there were seven pictures and one fifteen second video Dumont had recorded.

The pics were all of Farmer Howie's produce stand and the surrounding acreage except for one shot of two businessmen, one in a white shirt and red and blue striped tie and the other wearing tweedy tan sports jacket. Kyle knew the guy in the tie was Jack Dumont. He'd met him once. Phenomenal salesman with a real gift for connecting with people. The other guy was his closer, Mark something. They always tag-teamed their prospects. If Dumont and his closer couldn't pull it off, the deal couldn't be done. But, Kyle thought, how sweet would it be if I *could*?

The video was the real mystery—small red circles moving in a triangular motion over and over against the background of the produce stand. Kyle ran it again and again, zooming in as far as he could until he finally saw they were tomatoes.

Apparently juggling themselves.

༄

No shirt, Kyle thought as he drove up to the stand and saw Farmer Howie. Oh my fucking God, no shirt. And baggy, sagging tan cargo shorts with—help me, sweet Jesus—no hint of the Joe Boxers he wore yesterday. Holy fuck, he's freeballin'. As if to confirm that, Howie bent over to pick up a crate, the shorts riding down to show considerably more than the top of his pale ass crack. This is definitely going to make playing the tough guy a lot tougher, he thought.

Kyle pulled off to the side of the road and killed the engine. Farmer Howie straightened up and gave him a dopey, lopsided grin, waving as Kyle got out of the Explorer. The wave swayed his whole body, the baggy crotch of his shorts jiggling. Kyle could have sworn he saw the head of his cut dick swinging back and forth inside the fabric.

"What's the offer today?" he asked as Kyle approached.

Whatta goofball, Kyle thought. He's just a big puppy. "Well, I really don't have a better offer."

"No?"

"Nope. You won't sell it no matter how much I offer you, and I'm tired of looking like an idiot."

Farmer Howie grinned, pulling at a few hairs of his sparse beard before letting his fingers hook into the small gold chain he wore around his neck. "Soooo, you come to tell me you give up?"

"Not quite. Ever hear of eminent domain?"

He crossed his arms over his bare chest. "Sounds like one of them indie bands, but I don't get out to the clubs much since I moved here."

"Eminent domain," Kyle explained, "is a legal concept that basically means I can take your land away from you and use it for my own purposes provided the community agrees that it would generate more tax revenue in my hands than in yours."

Farmer Howie uncrossed his arms without a word and walked back to the produce stand. "Do you get that?" Kyle asked his tanned back.

"Yep," he replied, grabbing three tomatoes from the far bin and juggling them. Kyle flashed back to the video on Jack Dumont's cell phone, the hairs on his arm standing erect for a moment. Cheap goddamn company phones, he thought. Crap imaging technology. That's why the tomatoes looked like they were juggling themselves.

"And that doesn't worry you?"

Farmer Howie tracked the tomatoes with his eyes as he spoke. "Folks around here don't much like bein' told what's good for 'em. Especially by strangers."

"Beatrice at the Sand and Surf Motel will go for it. She's looking forward to the extra traffic the shopping center will bring in."

"M'kay, that's one. Who else you got lined up?"

"Nobody right now. But we haven't been to a town hall meeting to present our plans and profit projections yet. This land will be ours in six months, and you'll be back in Aspen schlepping snowboarders around the slopes. But it doesn't have to be that way. You can get a fair price and reopen your stand somewhere else. But you have to act quickly."

"Offer expires at midnight, huh?"

"Something like that."

He stopped juggling tomatoes, catching two in his right hand and one behind his back in his left. He put them back in the bin, propping one leg up on the wood.

"Hate to tell ya this, dude," he said, "but you'll never get that land. It ain't changin' hands on my watch. It'll be mine long after you're gone, doin' what it was meant to do—growing stuff. You go on and do what you have to. It'll be here next year givin' me tomatoes, corn, and strawberries. Land's blessed, dude. That's all I got to say." He turned his back on Kyle and squatted down, packing pint containers with strawberries from a big wicker basket.

I should have known that eminent domain shit wouldn't work, Kyle thought, but it was worth a shot. He craned his neck to peer down the gap between the farmer's cargo shorts and pale asscrack. *Fuck. What I wouldn't give to stick my finger down there and see what I come up with. Probably smells like strawberries.*

Plan B coming up.

⚜

THE NIGHT WAS perfect. A cool breeze ruffled the corn tassels, the sky was clear, the stars were bright, and the cicadas buzzed like a 10,000 megawatt lamp. A feeling of expectancy was in the air—as if the sky, the stars, the breeze and the bugs were all waiting for something to happen. And Kyle stood by the side of the road with a Bic lighter in his hand, making sure it would.

He had walked the three miles from the motel, lying low by the side of the road when a car came by so he wouldn't be seen. *It's got to look like an accident,* he thought. *People toss cigarette butts out their car windows all the time. A fire would be a shame—a tragedy even—but no great surprise. No more produce means no more produce stand, and Farmer Howie might think twice when sees the charred remains of his business smoking in the morning sun.*

He stepped into the rows of corn, shook a Marlboro out of the pack and cupped his hands to light it. He crouched down and applied the lit end of the cigarette to a dried cornstalk, but it wouldn't catch. Kyle frowned. He held it close to the stalk again but nothing happened. *That's weird,* he thought. He thumbed the lighter and took the flame right to the dry stalk, but it still wouldn't ignite. *What the fuck?* Kyle wondered. Then he heard a noise behind him.

Farmer Howie stood there grinning, his hair a crown of blonde that seemed even brighter in the full moon. "You're not gonna get that to burn," he said. "I told you before, dude, the land's blessed."

Kyle dropped the lighter and stood up. "What are you doing here?" he asked.

"My job. Something's up with the land. It told me, so here I am."

"Okay," Kyle said. "So, you caught me. What happens next?"

The farmer's high laugh seemed to come from everywhere. "What happens next? Well, I'm gonna give you something you've been wanting. Then, I'm gonna give you something you need."

He unsnapped his shorts and let them fall to the ground, his hard dick bobbing as he put his hands on Kyle's shoulders and forced him to kneel. Not that Kyle needed much forcing. *How did he know?* Kyle thought as he sank to his knees. *Have I been that obvious?*

All thoughts of obviousness, all the questions Kyle would normally have asked, vanished in the face of Farmer Howie's cock—just as Kyle had pictured it. About seven inches cut, with a beautifully formed helmet head. The thick, veiny shaft curved slightly to the right, its heft hovering over a smallish but low hanging pair of nuts. Kyle nuzzled them, smelling his musky ball sweat as he wrapped his hand around the farmer's dick and began working a pearl of precum around the head.

Farmer Howie moaned low and moved his hands from Kyle's shoulders to either side of his head. Kyle felt him position his dick close to his lips, and he opened them to receive the hanging host. It tasted salty and earthy and the farmer slowly fed it to Kyle, who deep throated it, amazed he could take as much as he did. He'd always had a pretty shallow gag reflex, but this seven inches slid down his throat with no problem.

He cupped Farmer Howie's balls, stroking his taint as he tightened his throat around his cock. The farmer began to rock and buck his hips against Kyle's face, bracing his hands on the back of Kyle's head as he dug his bare toes into the dirt. One loud groan later, Farmer Howie pumped his load down Kyle's throat, his hand keeping Kyle's head impaled on his dick. "Swallow," he commanded breathlessly, "don't spit. Can't waste the seed."

Kyle did as he was told, breathing through his nose as he gulped the farmer's cum. It tasted sweet—almost fruity—with a slight alcoholic aftertaste. With a final shudder, he leaned against Kyle's head and gave a satisfied sigh before he withdrew from his mouth. Kyle didn't want to let go, teasing and licking the head as Farmer Howie gently but firmly pulled up his shorts.

He bent over and grabbed Kyle by the shoulders, lifting him to his feet and embracing him roughly. Kyle melted into his bear hug like warm chocolate into a mold, letting the farmer kiss his neck. He opened his eyes and looked over the farmer's shoulder, noticing the scarecrows were closer. One of them had on a white shirt and a red and blue striped tie, and the other wore a ratty old tan tweed sports jacket with one long rip down the right sleeve. *Jesus Christ*, Kyle thought. Dumont and his closer. *They tag team their prospects.*

"Now comes what you need," Farmer Howie said as he pulled Kyle's face close and kissed him with smooth, soft lips. They sank into each others mouths, their tongues exploring wet darkness. The cicadas buzzed so loudly, Kyle almost didn't hear Farmer Howie's voice.

"Bite my tongue," he heard. "Bite it hard." But how could he speak? Kyle wondered. He would have had to pull away, but they hadn't stopped kissing. Crickets joined the cicadas, adding their voices to the background chorale. Kyle felt dizzy, overcome by the sensuality of the kiss, so he did as he was told. He bit, amazed to feel his teeth breaking the flesh.

"Yeah," he heard. "That's it. Bite it off." He couldn't stop himself. His teeth went through, and he sucked at the root until he felt it separate.

"Now chew it."

An explosion of strawberries filled his mouth as he began chewing. The flesh was tender and juicy, and the taste filled his head all the way down his throat and behind his eyes until he was dizzy and couldn't see. He couldn't feel the farmer or the kiss anymore. All he felt was strawberries and a vague sensation of falling.

He couldn't tell how long or far he'd fallen, but when he could see again, he found himself flat on his back in the cornfield. At least it looked like the same place—or did it? The stars seemed out of kilter, as if they'd been knocked them all out of the sky and rearranged. Cornstalks surrounded him, towering overhead like rustic skyscrapers.

The farmer was gone, but the scarecrows were at his head and feet now, Magic Marker grins splitting their faces of straw. But those grins were moving. Their mouths were opening, but nothing came out. They nodded to each other, then they picked Kyle up and turned him over on his stomach. He tried to scramble to his feet, but Dumont pushed his shoulders down while his closer raised Kyle's rear until he was on all fours.

With a desiccated rustling, Dumont grabbed Kyle's head in his two strong straw hands and slammed it roughly into the crotch of his torn jeans. Kyle tried to back away, but the hands held him fast and crushed his nose up against the buttons of the scarecrow's fly. He felt something growing, lumping up beneath the fabric.

He brought his hand up and felt around, partly out of curiosity and partly to relieve the pressure on his head. As soon as he touched the scarecrow's crotch, its chest rose and fell in a sigh and the hands let go of his head. And something definitely got harder under the jeans. *Oh man*, Kyle thought, *this is too fuckin' weird. But is it any weirder than anything else that's happened since I first saw this goddamn cornfield?*

Still dizzy, beyond curious and pretty horny after lusting after Farmer Howie for two days, Kyle couldn't believe he undid the buttons and reached inside. He didn't feel anything at first except the rasp of cornhusks abrading his palm, but on his second or third pass he felt a nub of something right between the scarecrow's legs. He applied pressure to it with his thumb and felt a moan coming from Dumont.

His hands caressed Kyle's head as he parted the fly and began rubbing the nub. It grew beneath his fingers, becoming longer and harder until Kyle finally bent his head down and licked at it. The scarecrow arched its back and pulled Kyle's head into the nub. His crotch smelled sweet yet fetid, like overripe fruit and rotting vegetable matter. The scent and the scene intoxicated Kyle. He really went to work then, teasing its smooth surface with his tongue, wetting it and blowing on it, lightly stroking the surrounding husks.

The nub had grown to a stalk about half the length of Kyle's index finger, more than enough to engulf with his lips. He sucked it and kissed it from tip to base and suddenly the tip split into a spray of fibers. Kyle nuzzled them, brushing them and pulling on them gently with his lips while the scarecrow ground his hips into Kyle's face.

Kyle took his hands and put them around Dumont's waist, pushing the jeans off his hips. As they fell to the ground, Kyle suddenly felt Dumont's closer reach around his own waist, unfasten his belt and pull his khakis down. The air felt cool and hot at the same time on his skin. He heard the clatter of his keys and cell phone as they slipped out of his pocket, but he made no move to pick them up.

Dumont's stalk kept growing, the tassels in a sensual tangle with Kyle's tongue like anemone fingers. Coarse straw hands slid Kyle's boxer briefs off his ass and parted his hairy cheeks. Kyle's dick stiffened in response. Dumont's closer reached around and began to milk it. A crackling rustle of leaves came from behind Kyle as he felt the scarecrow lower himself to his knees. Something bristly grazed Kyle's ass. He couldn't tell if it was a hand or a tongue. Did they *have* tongues? he wondered.

Whatever it was, Kyle loved what it was doing. It was bristly, then it was rough, then it was slick, then it was all three—rimming him delicately then running up and down the length of his asscrack with long, broad strokes. He didn't want to cum yet, so he pushed the hand away and concentrated on the blowjob he was about to give.

Dumont's cock stalk was about six inches long, and the fibers had stopped dueling Kyle's tongue, making way for a warm, fleshy pillar that slid slickly out of the stalk. Kyle thought it looked like an ear of corn with its kernels flattened. It tasted sweet and sticky. As he sucked on it, the scarecrow's breath came quick and shallow. Kyle automatically raised a hand to cup his balls, but none hung there.

At the same time Kyle noticed an absence under his hand, he sensed a presence close to his ass. The hairs of his crack were being matted down by a stalk as slimy as the one slamming in and out of his mouth. With little prelude, Dumont's closer slipped smoothly inside Kyle and began fucking him with long, slow thrusts. The straw scratched Kyle's cheeks as the scarecrow buried himself deep inside.

They sandwiched Kyle, moving in a rhythm that threatened to squeeze the breath out of him. Silently pounding him from the front and back, they pumped faster and faster, their viscous syrup dripping down Kyle's chin and running down the backs of his thighs. His mouth and ass were numb. He couldn't even tell if his dick was still hard or not, and he didn't much care.

The motion became frantic, both scarecrows hammering away at him, puddles forming below his mouth and between his legs. Lost in a sea of sweet sweat, Kyle felt his own load building up. I'm gonna shoot without even touching my cock, he thought. But before he could, the two scarecrows issued the first sounds he actually heard from them.

They weren't the moans of passion he'd been expecting. They weren't moans at all but more like wails. And those wails carried a note of welcome, as if he now had something in common with them. When the last note had been borne away on the breeze, the scarecrows vanished and Kyle was left in a puddle of ooze.

He tried to get up, but he couldn't stand. He was dizzy, and their juices leaked from him. He felt full, plump with their seed even though he hadn't felt them cum. Sinking back down, his head fell into the slimy pool, too heavy to hold up. The stars began swirling again. Kyle grasped the surrounding vegetation, trying to stop the field from spinning out of control, but stability slipped through his fingers. He felt like he was falling again—past the rows of corn, past the rotting husks, past the slime and the stars, past the farmer and the scarecrows, past space and time, past his own body until it stripped itself away from his soul.

Which fell even further.

※

THE SUN SHONE warm and strong on the cornfield. It's gonna be hot today, Kyle thought. He watched the farmer as he waited on a couple of carloads of tourists parked at the produce stand across the road. Even farther away in the field, he saw the two scarecrows staring back at him at eye level. The sunlight glinted on the face of his gold Rolex, which was now strapped to a wrist of straw. He couldn't blink. He couldn't talk. He couldn't move, but it didn't matter. Along with Dumont and his closer, he had to keep watch over the fields and the farmer. That was his job now. Farmer Howie had been right all along.

The land *was* blessed.

AFTERWORD

GREEDY, DEVIANT AND PERVERSE: LIVING AND WRITING A TRIO RELATIONSHIP

REDFERN JON BARRETT

THERE ARE NO blueprints for being in a three-way relationship. There are few self-help books, novels, movies, role models, or even greetings cards for those with two partners. Friends will not have helpful advice, and the best relatives will be able to offer is a confused and tentative support. You won't have any good examples to emulate or mimic, nor will you have any bad ones to learn from. To be in a three-way relationship is to feel your way around in the dark. For those with two lovers in the early 21st Century, it is *you* who will be the role model for those coming after.

If that sounds like a responsibility, it is. As with most gay people just a couple of decades ago, you will find yourself to be the ambassador to everyone you know: those friends of yours may not have advice, but they will have plenty of questions; those family members will be providing judgement alongside that support. You will likely be the first three-way bond for people you meet at parties, on dating sites, and on social media. Without commonplace polyamorous books and movies, you guys will be the ones representing 'throuples', 'triads', and 'trios' everywhere.

This also affords opportunities offered to few others: without rules and guidelines, you're free to make your own. Without the centuries of social conditioning provided to monogamous relationships, you can shape and form things as the three of you wish. Without the ghosts of generations past offering themselves as an example, you're provided with a flexibility few will ever get to know. You may be fumbling in the dark (in more ways than one), but as long as the three of you are happy, there is no right or wrong way to go about your trio.

Yet pioneers can only go so far. Acceptance and understanding toward those in polyamorous relationships will only be reached with greater cultural visibility. Empathy comes alongside knowledge, and so people need sympathetic examples they can relate to. Our stories need to be told because ignorance drives the hatred which many of us receive on a regular basis. All too often we are called greedy. We are called deviants and perverts. Without concrete examples of love between three people, the public are left with the worst recesses of their imaginations.

For polyamorous authors this means a double responsibility: in both our personal and professional lives we're trying to convey a type of relationship most are still unfamiliar with. In our private lives this simply means being yourself and allowing others to see that the three of you are making each other happy—that three people really can love one another and that in doing so the world won't end. Yet for an author things are not so simple. How does one create tales of three-way love which people will want to read?

The story of my partners and I would make for a poor novel or short story. Darren and I had been together for a few years before we slowly opened up our relationship, taking things a step at a time until we found ourselves straight-out dating other guys. Rather than causing drama, we each found 'compersion'—the feeling of joy from seeing someone you care about being made happy by someone else (that is, the opposite of jealousy). We've been together almost a decade, and things have always been peaceful and content. When Alex came along we welcomed him into our lives and he wound up moving in. It was relatively straightforward, and, though exciting to us, it would be unlikely to prove gripping to those browsing bookstores or patronising movie theatres.

Writing three-way relationships which are both realistic, sympathetic, and entertaining is no easy task, yet collections such as this could not be more important to expanding the public's view of what is possible in the world of love and sex. To convey the magic in the mundanity, the excitement in ordinary people forming unusual families and love affairs. After all, all art is propaganda, and those in polyamorous relationships are in sore need of visibility.

It is no surprise that it is LGBT publishers which are pushing these boundaries. Having so often been at the forefront of social change—long before their larger, better-funded heterosexual counterparts catch up—the queer publishing industry has for decades provided a voice to those who would otherwise lack one. On this I am certainly biased: my first published novel was released by Lethe Press, who took a chance on a tale about (you guessed it) a three-way love affair. LGBT publishing houses are all too aware of the importance of spreading stories, and without them it is unlikely I could have shared my own.

There are no blueprints for being in a three-way relationship. There are few self-help books, novels, movies, role models, or even greetings cards for those with two partners. But with each passing year there are more. For every novel, TV show, and short story which shows our lives, our culture gets a little richer, and the lives of those different to the norm become a little bit easier. It is stories which provide us with hope for the future, and which for each new generation drive change the previous would scarcely have believed possible. Ultimately it is stories in which we find freedom—especially for us greedy, deviant, and perverse people with two boyfriends.

—Redfern Jon Barrett

ABOUT THE AUTHORS

SHANE ALLISON's editing career began with the best-selling gay erotic anthology *Hot Cops: Gay Erotic Stories*, and he has gone on to publish over a dozen gay erotica anthologies such as *Straight Guys: Gay Erotic Fantasies*, *Cruising: Gay Erotic Stories*, *Middle Men: Gay Erotic Threesomes*, *Frat Boys: Gay Erotic Stories*, *Brief Encounters: 69 Hot Gay Shorts*, *College Boys: Gay Erotic Stories*, *Hardworking Men: Gay Erotic Fiction*, *Hot Cops: Gay Erotic Fiction*, *Backdraft: Fireman Erotica*, and *Afternoon Pleasures: Erotica for Gay Couples*. Shane Allison has appeared in five editions of *Best Gay Erotica*, *Best Black Gay Erotica* and *Zane's Z-Rated: Chocolate Flava 3*. His debut poetry collection, *Slut Machine* is out from Queer Mojo and his poem/memoir *I Remember* is out from Future Tense Books. His debut novel *You're the One That I Want* is forthcoming from Strebor Books in 2016. Shane is hard at work on his next novel and currently resides in Tallahassee, Florida.

Born in the north of England in 1984, REDFERN JON BARRETT is a polyamorous pagan giant with a Ph.D. in queer literature. He is the author of *The Giddy Death of the Gays and the Strange Demise of the Straights* and *Forget Yourself* (both from Lethe Press). His shorter fiction has featured in the magazines *A Cappella Zoo*, *The Future Fire*, *Sleek*, and *Corvus*; the anthologies *Bestiary*, *Drag Noir*, and *Heiresses of Russ*; as well as the book *Shaped by Time*. His non-fiction has featured in German newspapers *Bild* and *BZ*, as well as *Scifi Methods*, *Gender Forum*, *Polytical*, *Überlin*, and *Witches/Sorcières*.

Born and raised in Chicago, N.S. BERANEK holds a Bachelor of Arts degree in Technical Theater and Design, and for nineteen years was an Assistant Propmaster in regional theatre. Previous stories have appeared in *Best Gay Romance 2014* (Cleis Press), *Diverse Voices Quarterly*, vol. 6 issue 21, and *Saints*

& Sinners: New Fiction from the Festival (Bold Strokes Books) 2013, 2014, and 2015. A novel, *Bardo*, will be released by Lethe Press in 2016.

EVEY BRETT lives in Southern Arizona with two cats, a snake and her Lipizzan mare, Carrma, who has a habit of arranging the universe to her liking. Evey has attended the Clarion Writer's Workshop for SF/F, The Taos Toolbox workshop, the Lambda Literary Retreat for Emerging LGBT Authors and has an MA in Writing Popular Fiction from Seton Hill University. Published by Lethe Press, Cleis Press, Loose Id, Ellora's Cave and elsewhere, Evey is the author of numerous paranormal and fantasy stories under this name and two others. Visit her online at **eveybrett.wordpress.com**.

'NATHAN BURGOINE lives in Ottawa with his husband. His first novel *Light* was a finalist for a Lambda Literary Award. 'Nathan's shorts appear in dozens of publications, including *This Is How You Die*, *Foolish Hearts* and *A Family By Any Other Name*. Find him online at **nathanburgoine.com**.

DALE CHASE has written male erotica for eighteen years, her work published in magazines, anthologies, and story collections. She has two western novels in print plus her latest release *Hot Copy: Classic Gay Erotica from the Magazine Era*, from Lethe Press. She is presently at work on her next novel, *Hot Pursuit*, about a pair of cowboy detectives working out of a San Francisco agency in 1874. A California native, Chase lives near San Francisco.

CHRIS COLBY is a pseudonym. As such, his likes, country of residence, amount of pets and marital status are hard to verify. It is rumoured that the poet Mark Ward, based in Dublin, Ireland has more information about his identity but Mark cannot be located at this time. When we rang Mark's voicemail, a cryptic message (once reversed) hinted that there may be more information at **astintinyourspotlight.wordpress.com** regarding Chris' identity and Mark's whereabouts.

LAWRENCE JACKSON is the author of two fantastical erotic novels, *Misadventure in Space and Time* and *Muscle Worshipers*. 'The Big Match' is his first published work in a realist mode, but he does have a story in an upcoming anthology featuring no time travel or telepathy whatsoever. However, he has just embarked on a new erotic adventure featuring the lost city of Atlantis. He lives in South London and is on Twitter as **@lawrencewrites.**

JEFF MANN has published three poetry chapbooks, five full-length books of poetry, two collections of personal essays, a volume of memoir and poetry, three novellas, four novels, and two collections of short fiction. He teaches creative writing at Virginia Tech in Blacksburg, Virginia.

ROB ROSEN (**therobrosen.com**) is the award-winning author of the novels *Sparkle: The Queerest Book You'll Ever Love*, *Divas Las Vegas*, *Hot Lava*, *Southern Fried*, *Queerwolf*, *Vamp*, *Queens of the Apocalypse*, *Creature Comfort* and *Fate*, and editor of the anthologies *Lust in Time*, *Men of the Manor* and *Best Gay Erotica 2015* and *2016*, and has had short stories featured in more than 200 anthologies.

ROBERT RUSSIN was born and raised in the Bronx and has a hard time being anywhere else. Because of thirty years of poor choices he is still a waiter and tries to write stories in the downtime between filling glasses and clearing dishes. For obvious reasons these stories tend to be sad and devoid of all hope. He prefers ice cream to men, but will sometimes write about sex.

JERRY L. WHEELER is a three-time Lambda Literary Award finalist as both editor and author. His fiction and non-fiction has appeared in a number of anthologies, including his collection of short stories and essays, *Strawberries and Other Erotic Fruits* (Lethe Press, 2012).

ABOUT THE EDITOR

MATTHEW BRIGHT is a writer, editor and designer who often wonders in what order those words should be. His short fiction has appeared in *Queers Destroy Horror (Nightmare Magazine)*, *Queen Mob's Teahouse*, *Revolutions: Manchester Speculative Fiction*, *The Biggest Lover* and *Men in Love*. With the poet Christopher Black, he is the co-author of the experimental novella *Between The Lines*. Wearing the editor hat, alongside this volume he is also the editor of dark-queer anthology *The Myriad Carnival* and forthcoming titles *Gents* and *Clockwork Cairo*. By day, he pays the bills as a cover designer at INKSPIRAL DESIGN. He lives in Manchester, England with his partner John, and a dog with a taste for eating valuable hardback books. Find him on twitter at **@mbrightwriter** or online at **matthew-bright.com**.

(If this sort of thing is of interest to you, the eponymous song featured in 'Time To Dance' is by The Jezabels, from their 2013 album *The Brink*.)

CPSIA information can be obtained
at www.ICGtesting.com
Printed in the USA
BVHW032107030820
585401BV00001B/75